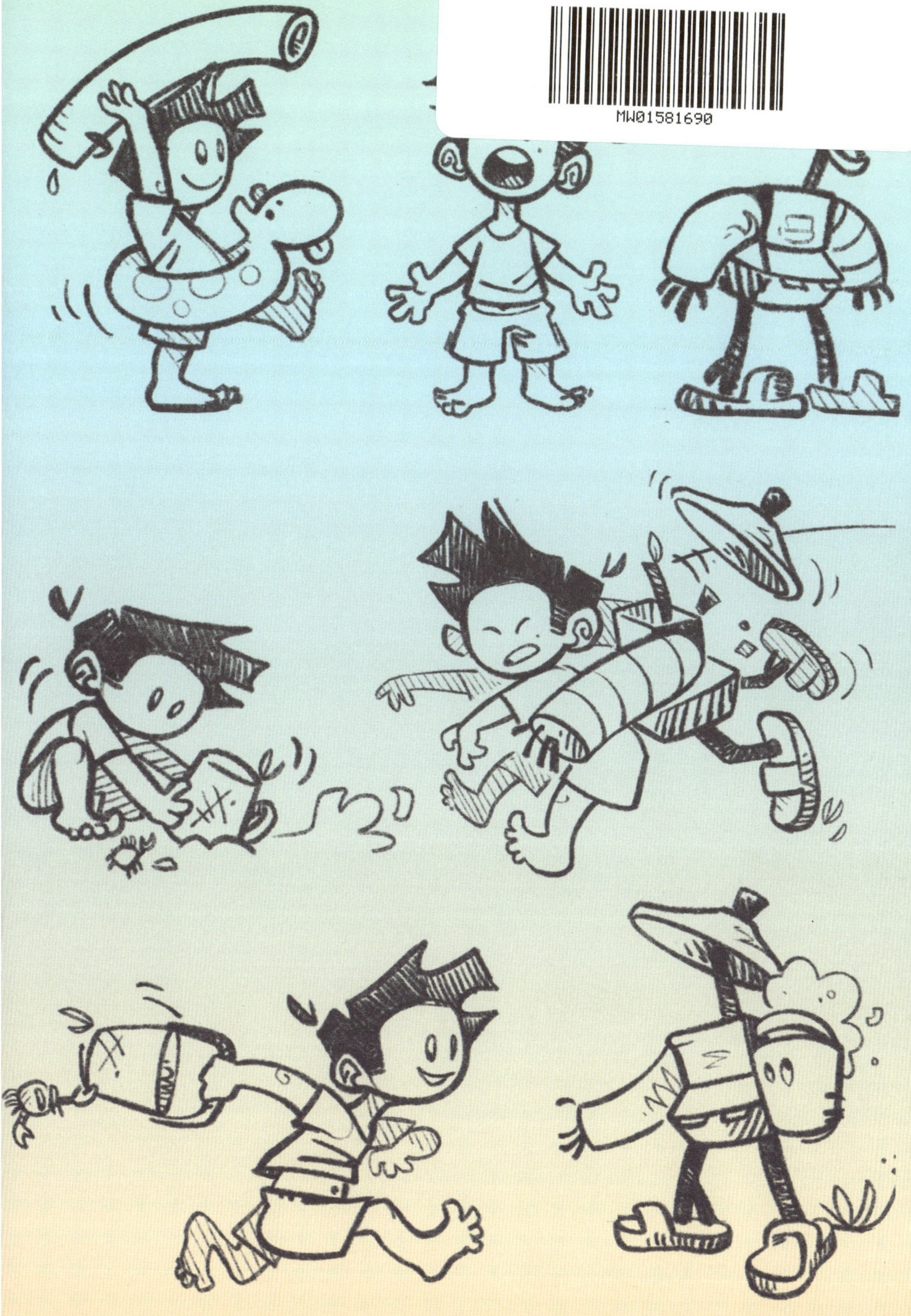

HAKU and SAM

A graphic adventure in Hawai'i

> Come on, Sam!

Shane Petosa-Sigel

BeachHouse

Copyright © 2022 by BeachHouse Publishing

No part of this book may be reproduced in any form or by any electronic or mechanical means, including information storage and retrieval devices or systems, without prior written permission from the publisher, except that brief passages may be quoted for reviews.
All rights reserved.

ISBN 978-1-949000-222-1
Library of Congress Control Number: 2022930909
First Printing, May 2022

BeachHouse Publishing, LLC
PO Box 5464 • Kāneʻohe, Hawaiʻi 96744
info@beachhousepublishing.com • www.beachhousepublishing.com

Printed in South Korea

Table of Contents

1. Making Friends • 4

2. Bucket Head • 12

3. Party Crasher • 21

4. Getting Ahead • 32

5. Unpacking • 44

6. Back Home • 53

chapter one

MAKING FRIENDS

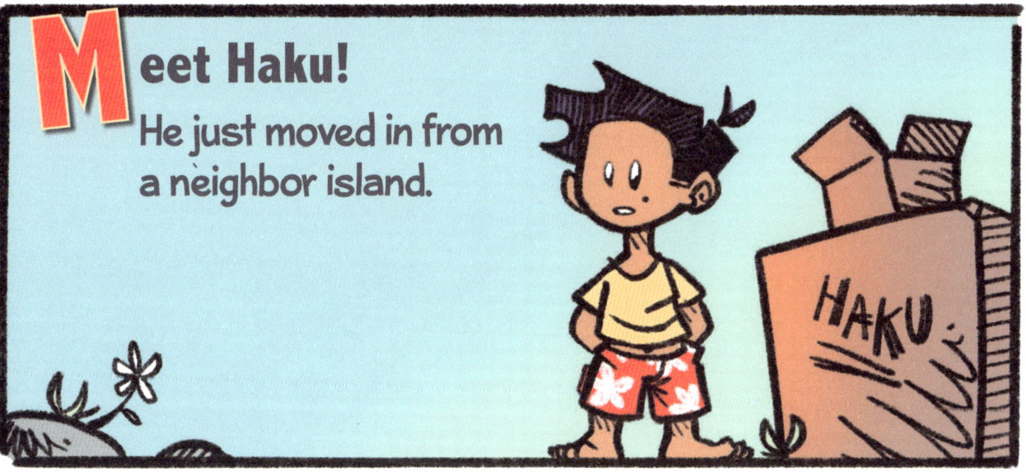
Meet Haku!
He just moved in from a neighbor island.
HAKU

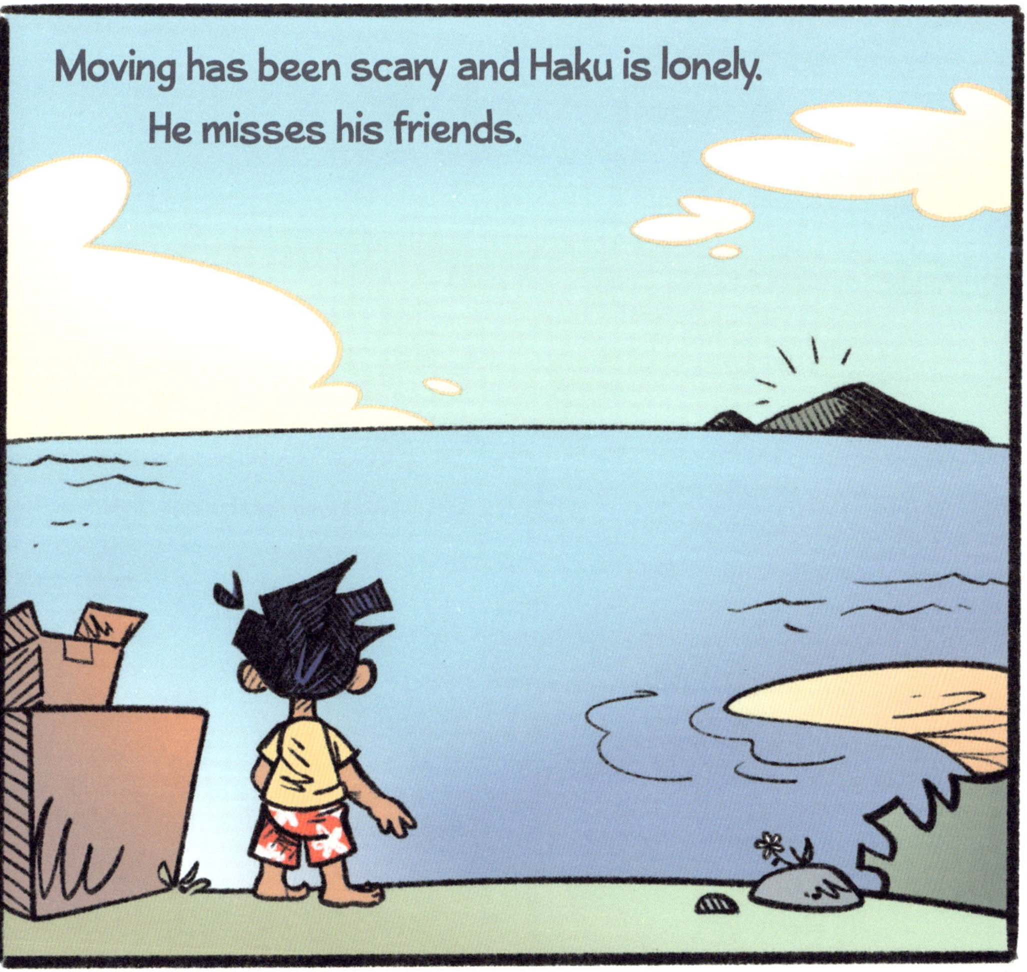
Moving has been scary and Haku is lonely.
He misses his friends.

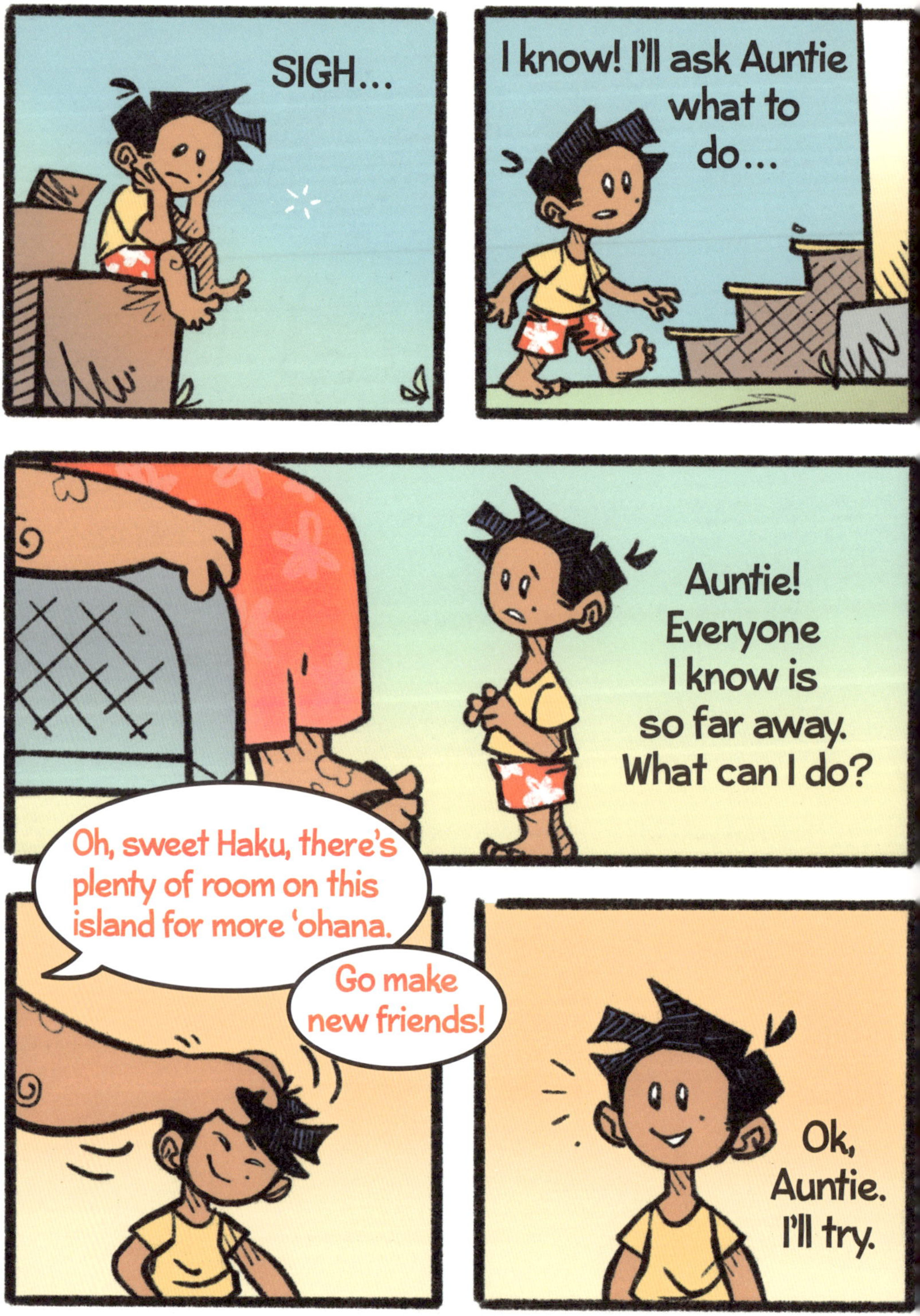
SIGH...
I know! I'll ask Auntie what to do...
Auntie! Everyone I know is so far away. What can I do?
Oh, sweet Haku, there's plenty of room on this island for more 'ohana.
Go make new friends!
Ok, Auntie. I'll try.

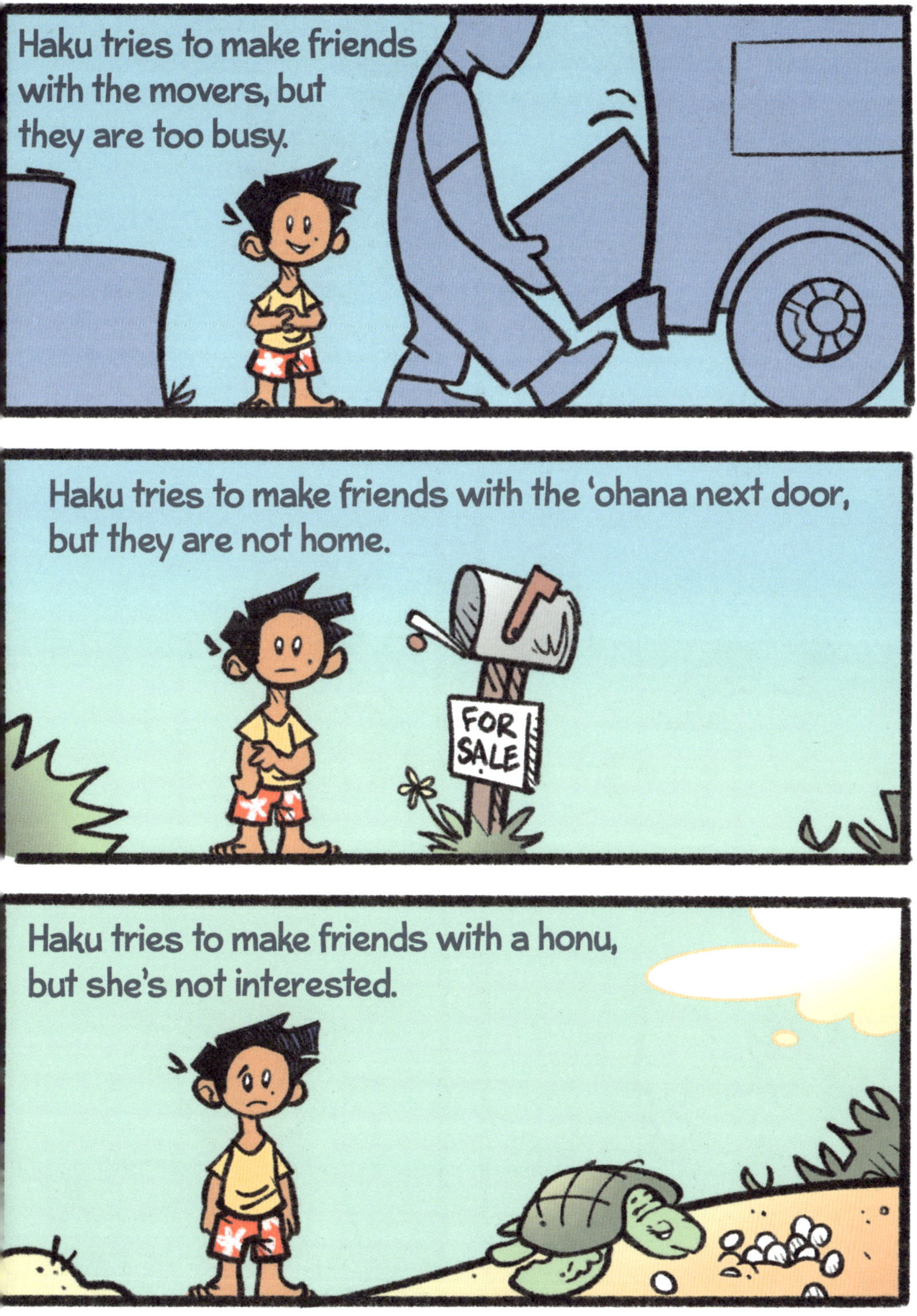
Haku tries to make friends with the movers, but they are too busy.
Haku tries to make friends with the ‘ohana next door, but they are not home.
FOR SALE
Haku tries to make friends with a honu, but she's not interested.

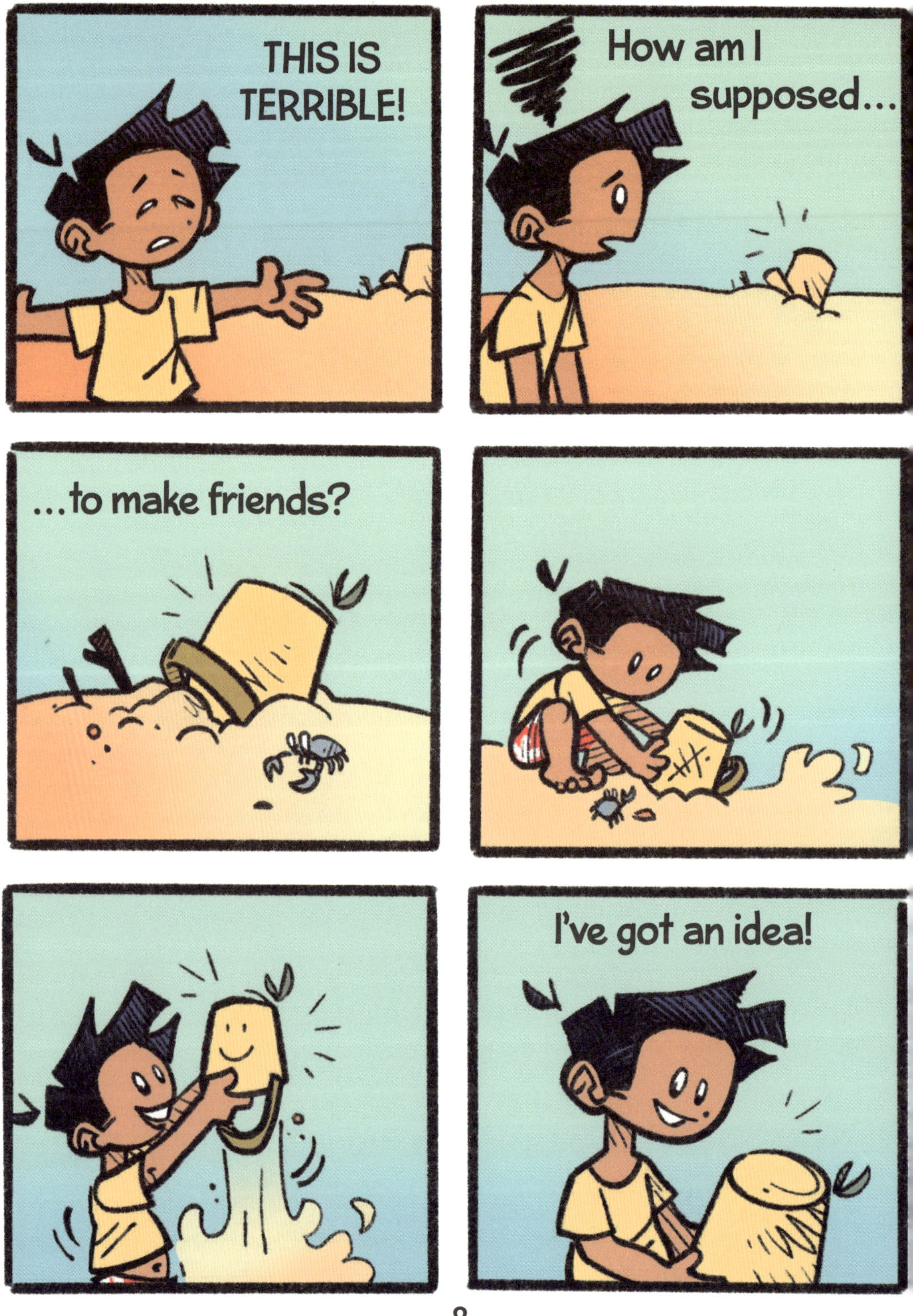
THIS IS TERRIBLE!
How am I supposed...
...to make friends?
I've got an idea!

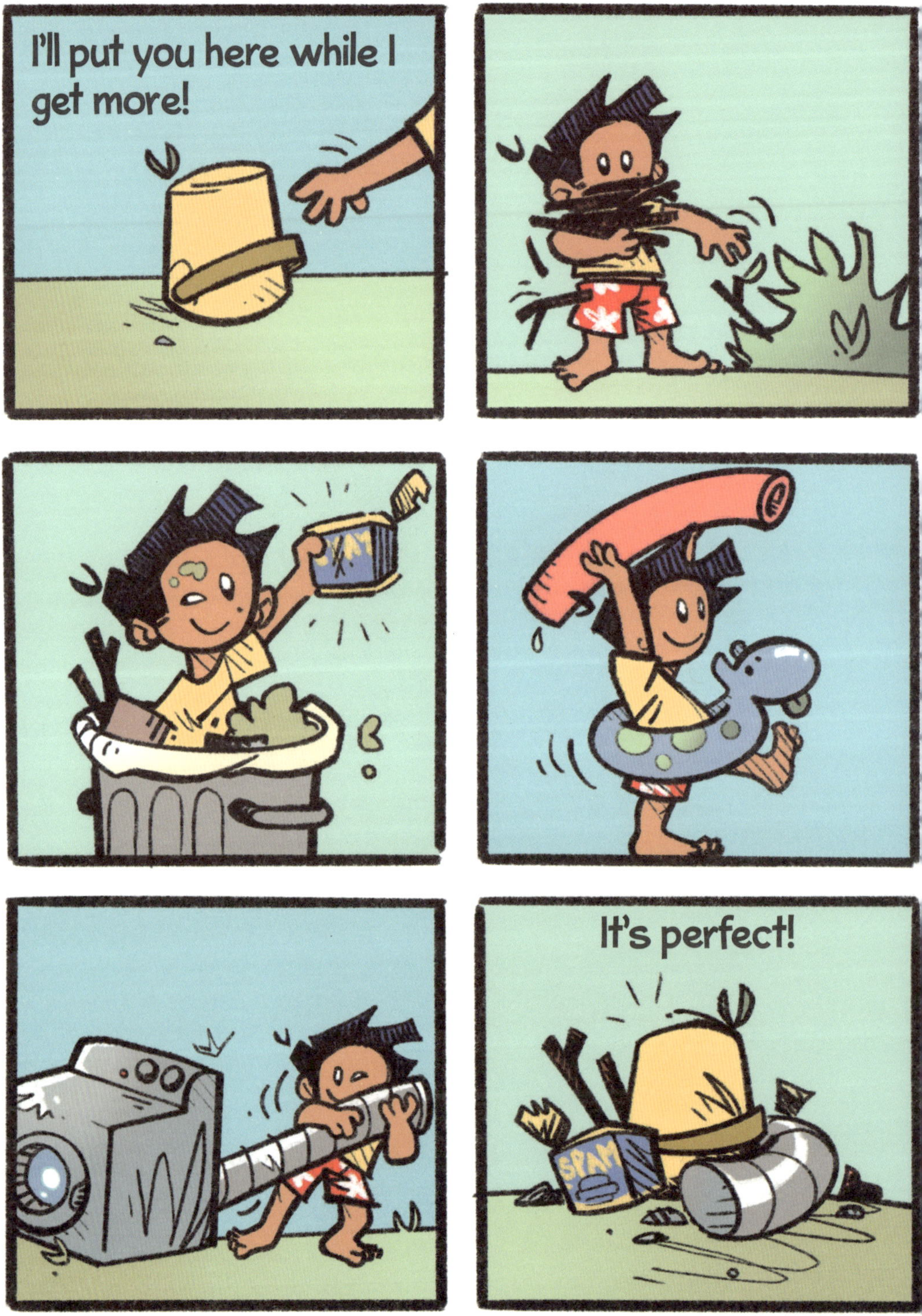
I'll put you here while I get more!
SPAM
SPAM
It's perfect!

Wait till Auntie sees my new friend!

chapter two

BUCKET HEAD

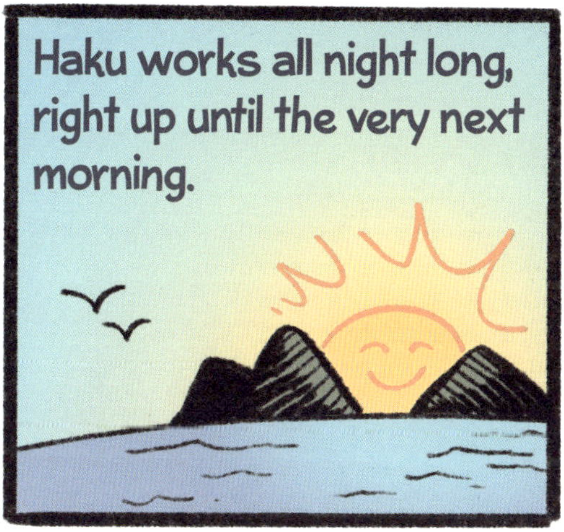
Haku works all night long, right up until the very next morning.

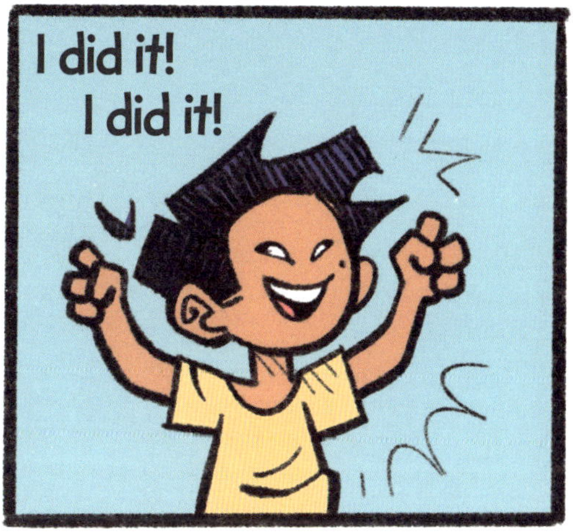
I did it!
I did it!

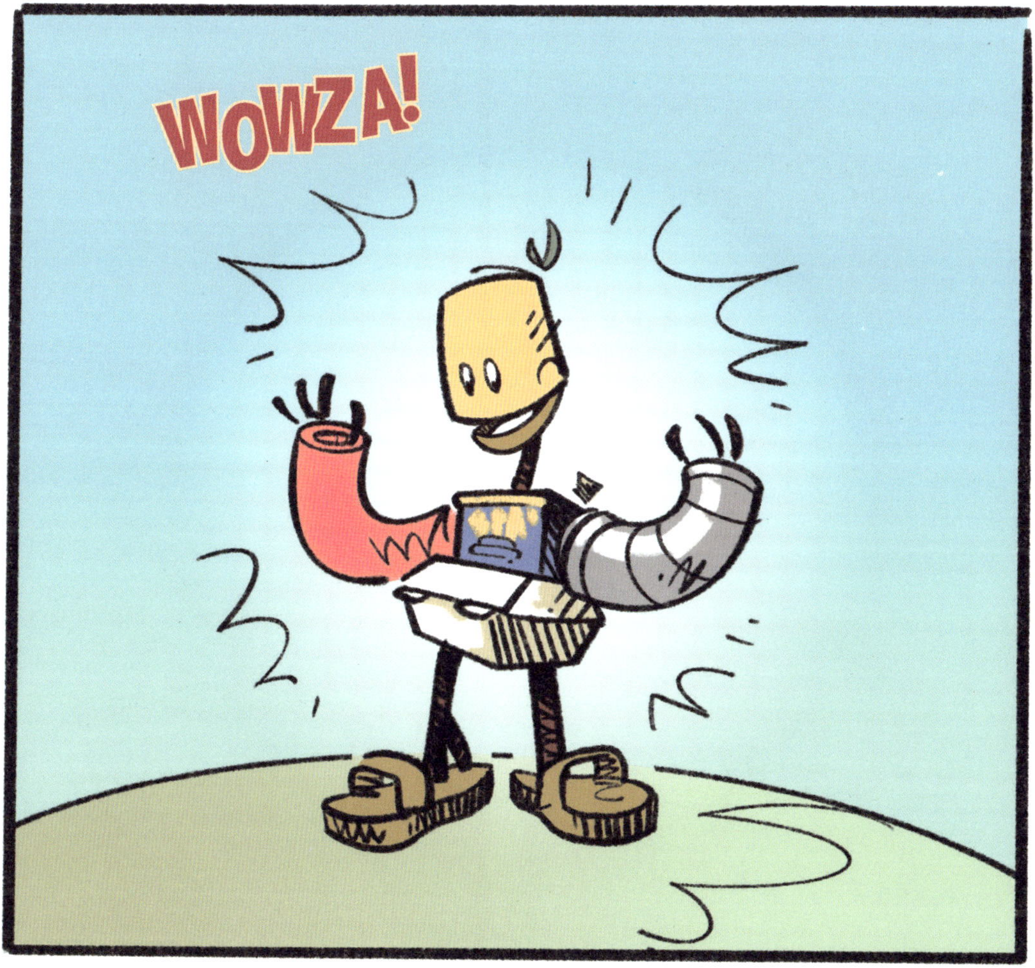
WOWZA!

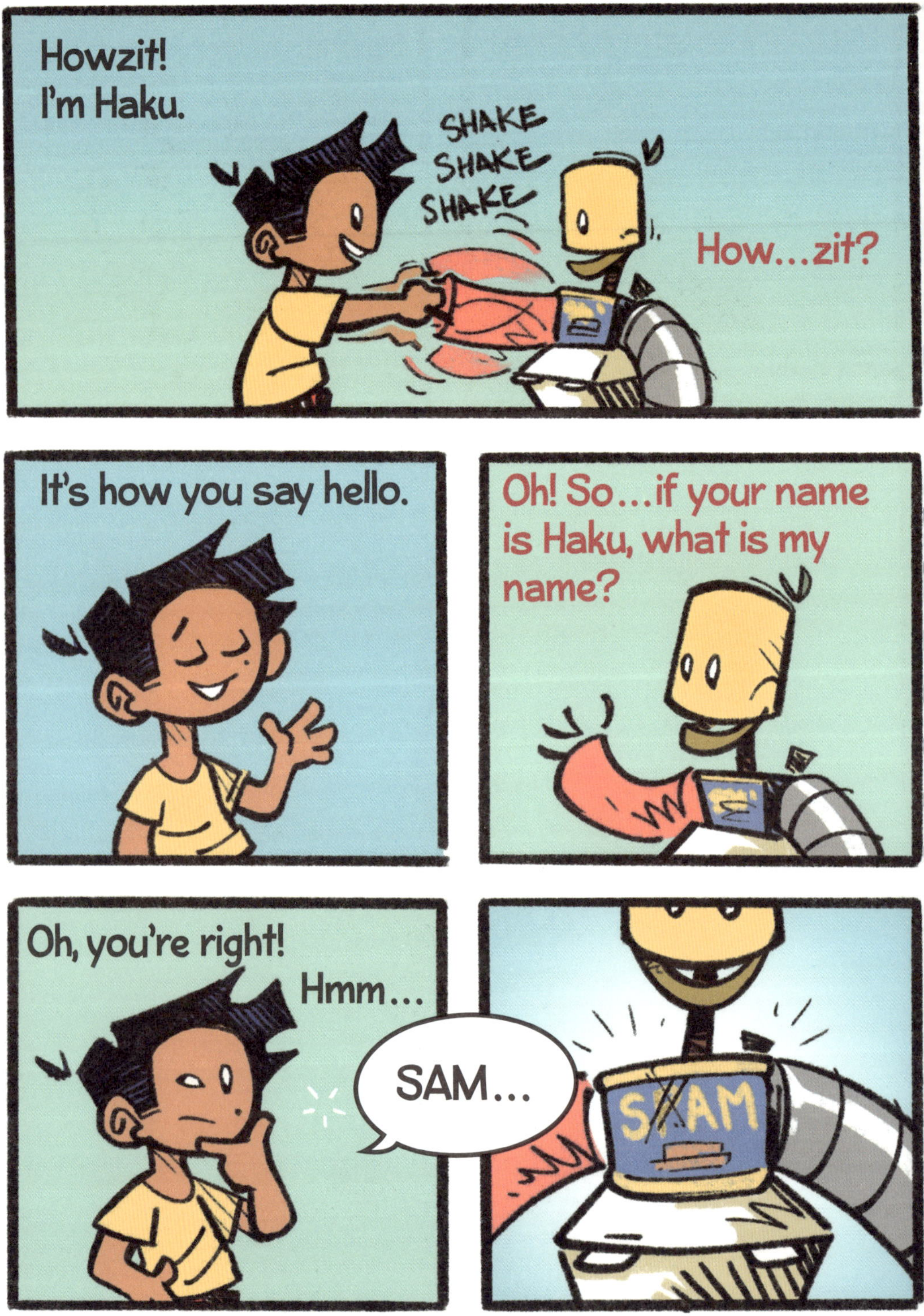

Howzit!
I'm Haku.
SHAKE
SHAKE
SHAKE
How...zit?
It's how you say hello.
Oh! So...if your name is Haku, what is my name?
Oh, you're right!
Hmm...
SAM...
SPAM

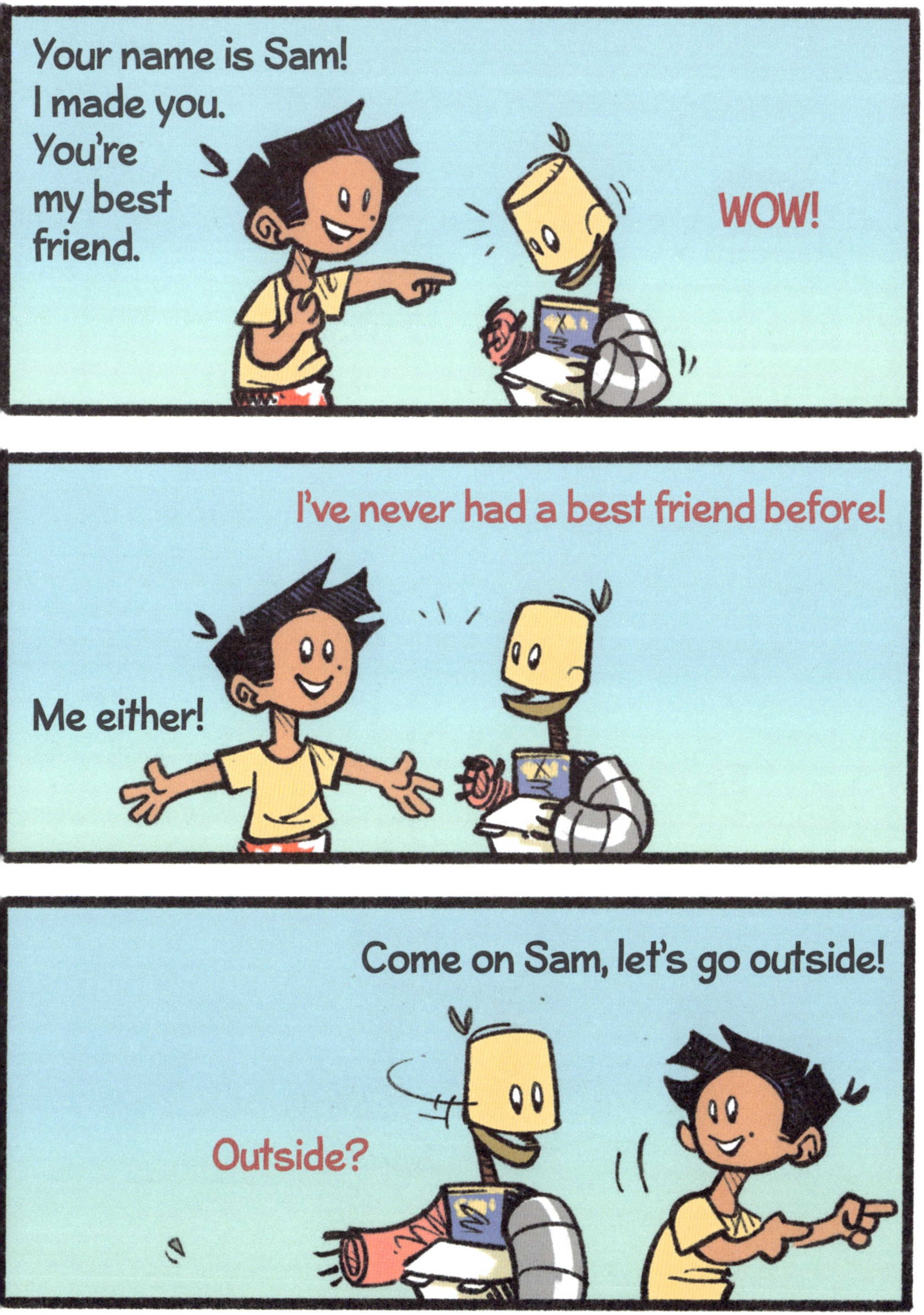
Your name is Sam! I made you. You're my best friend.
WOW!
I've never had a best friend before!
Me either!
Come on Sam, let's go outside!
Outside?

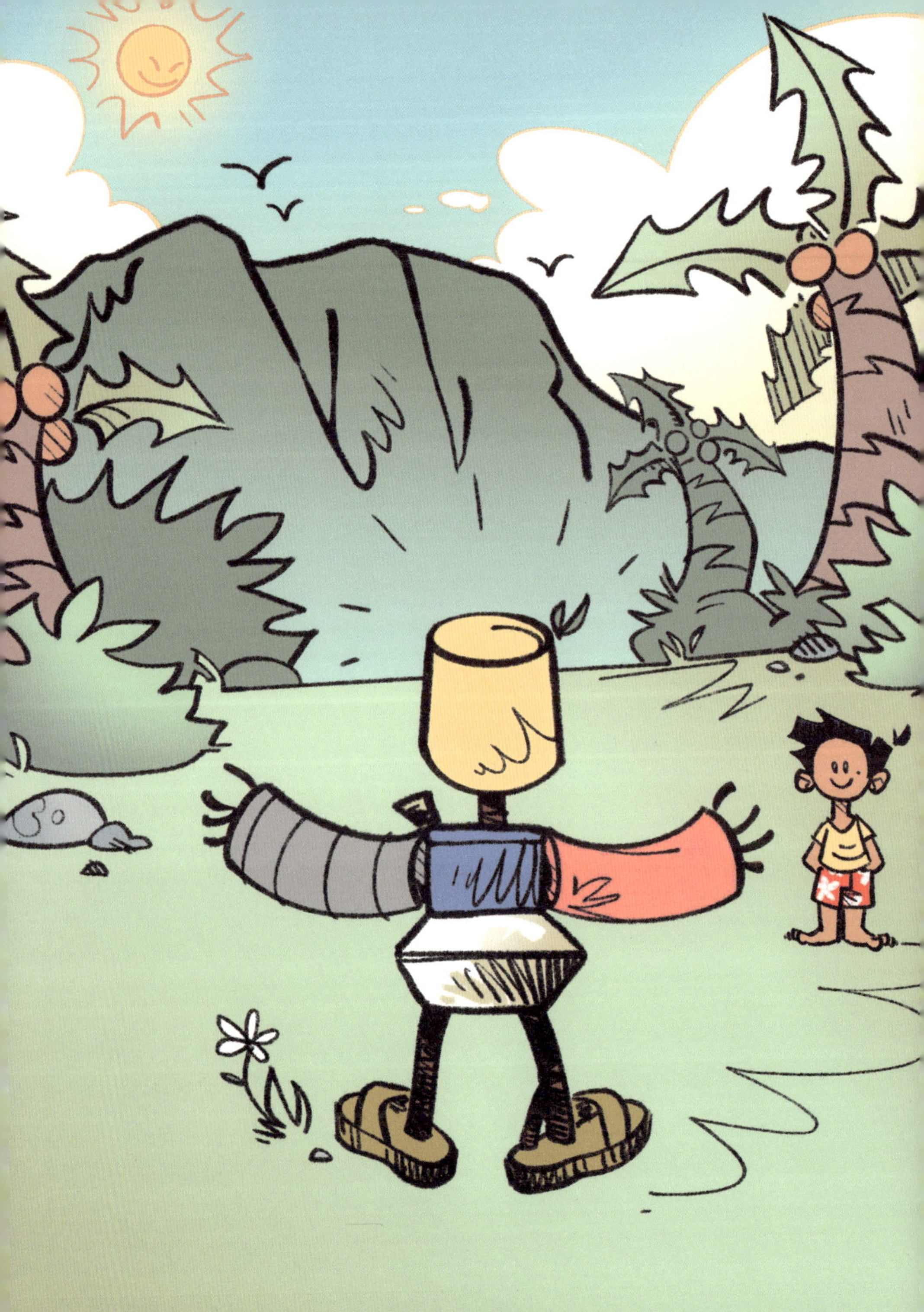

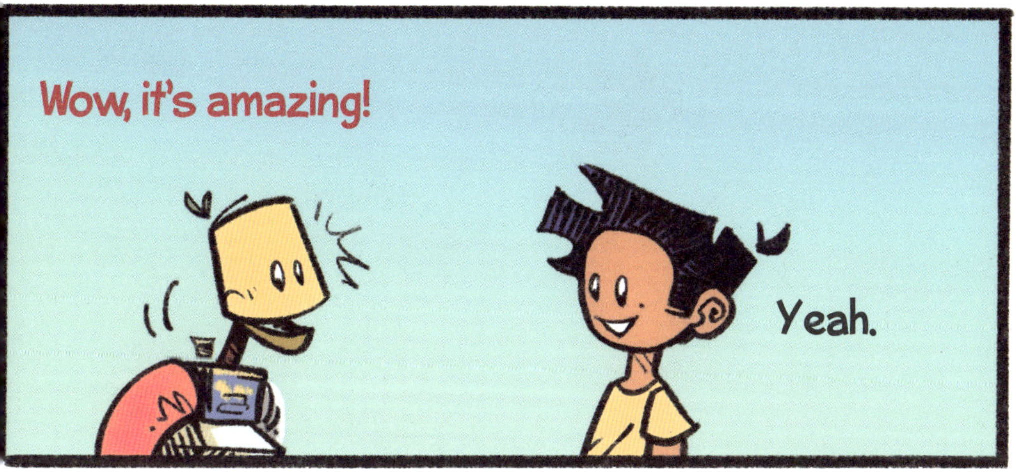
Wow, it's amazing!
Yeah.

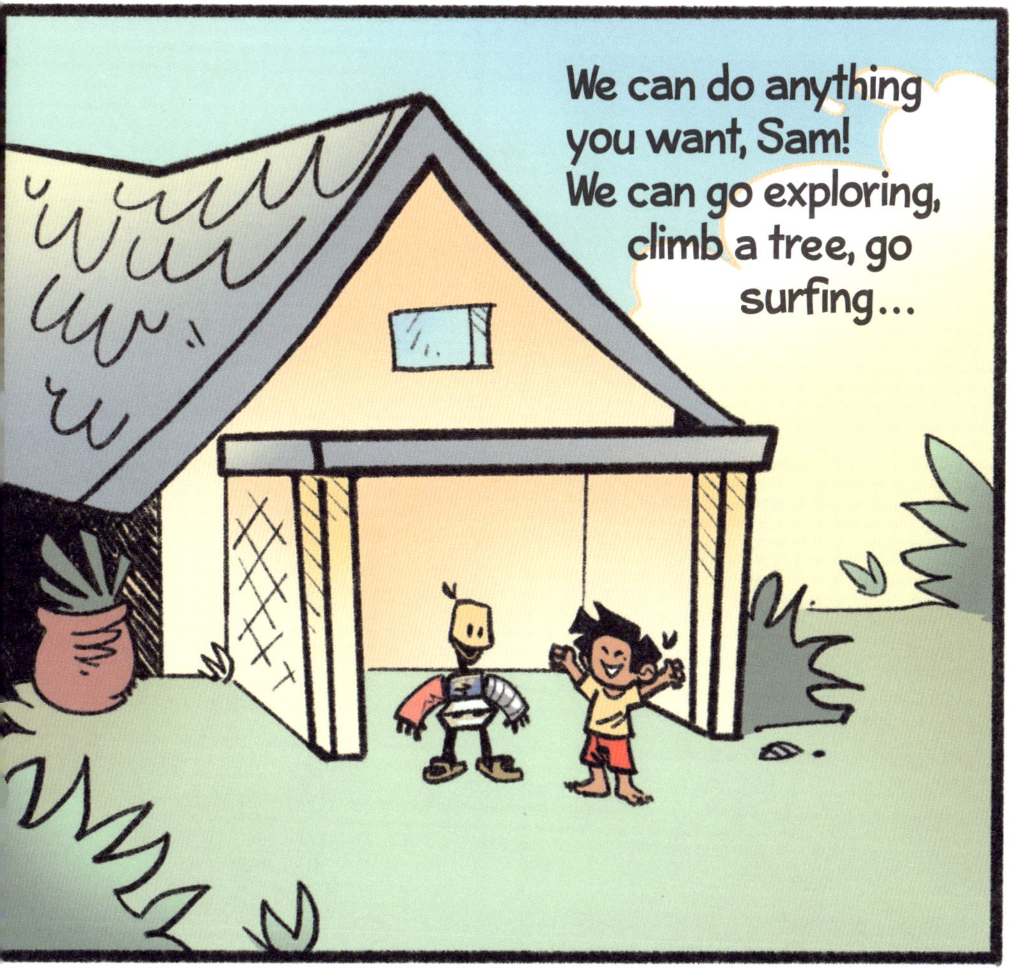
We can do anything you want, Sam! We can go exploring, climb a tree, go surfing...

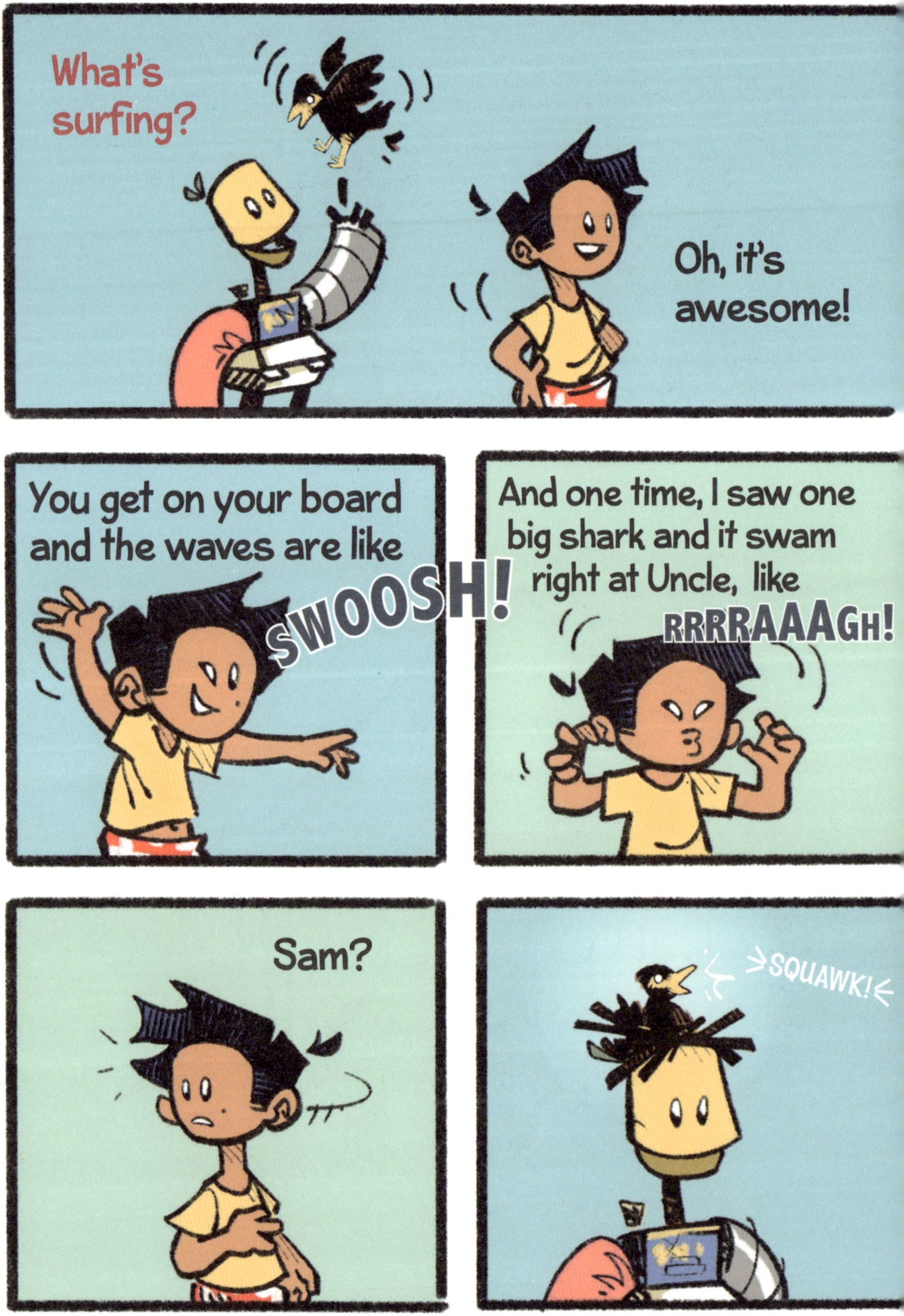
What's surfing?
Oh, it's awesome!
You get on your board and the waves are like
SWOOSH!
And one time, I saw one big shark and it swam right at Uncle, like
RRRRAAAGH!
Sam?
SQUAWK!

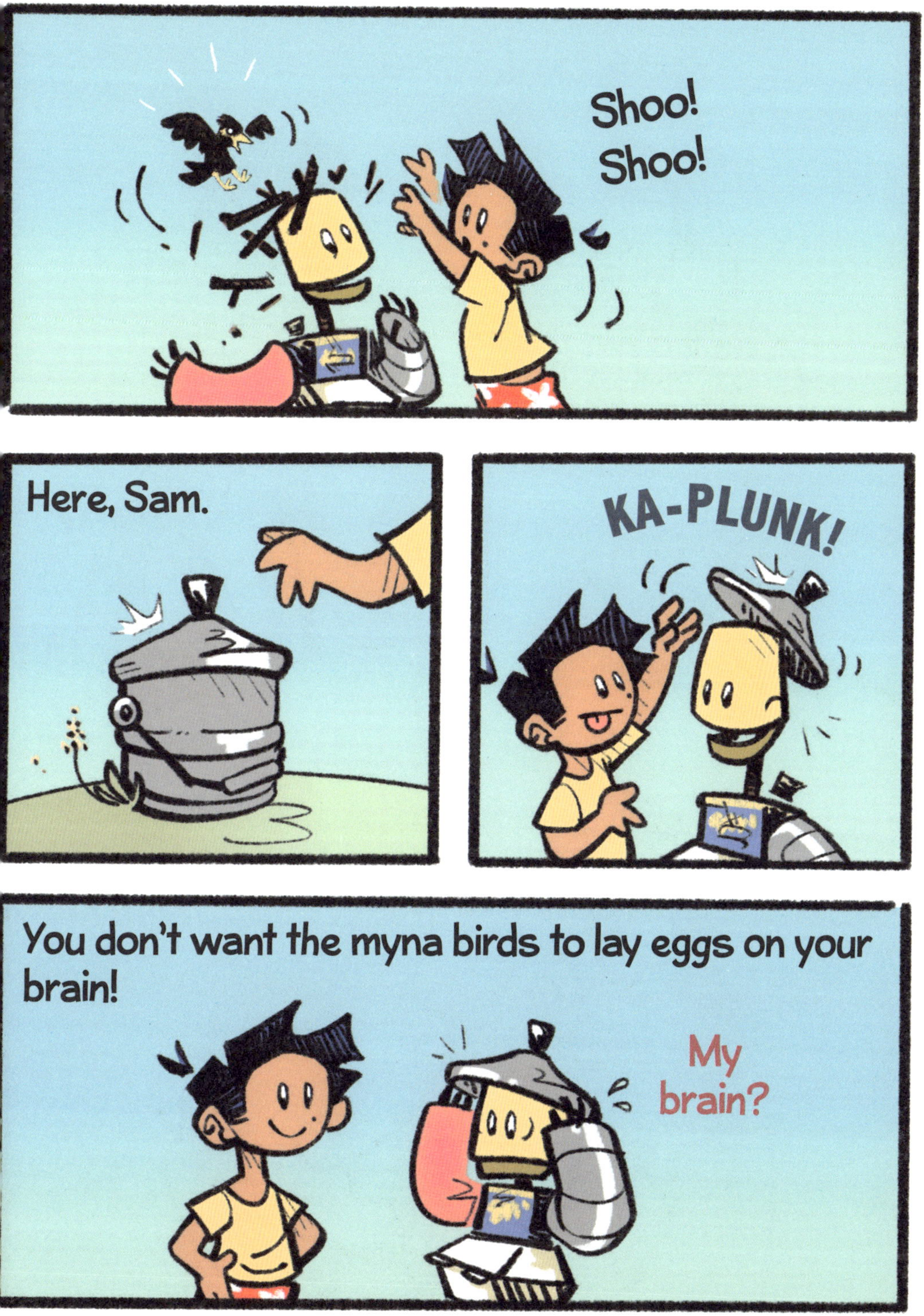
Shoo!
Shoo!
Here, Sam.
KA-PLUNK!
You don't want the myna birds to lay eggs on your brain!
My brain?

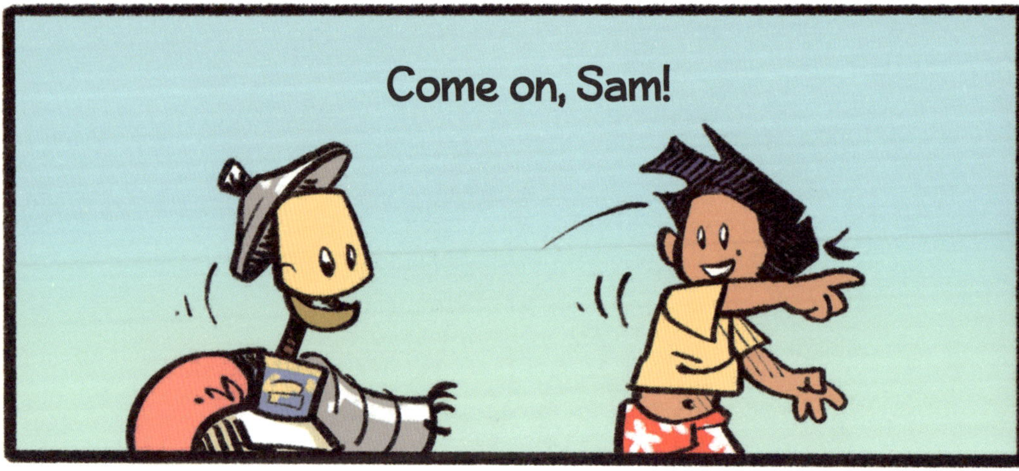
Come on, Sam!

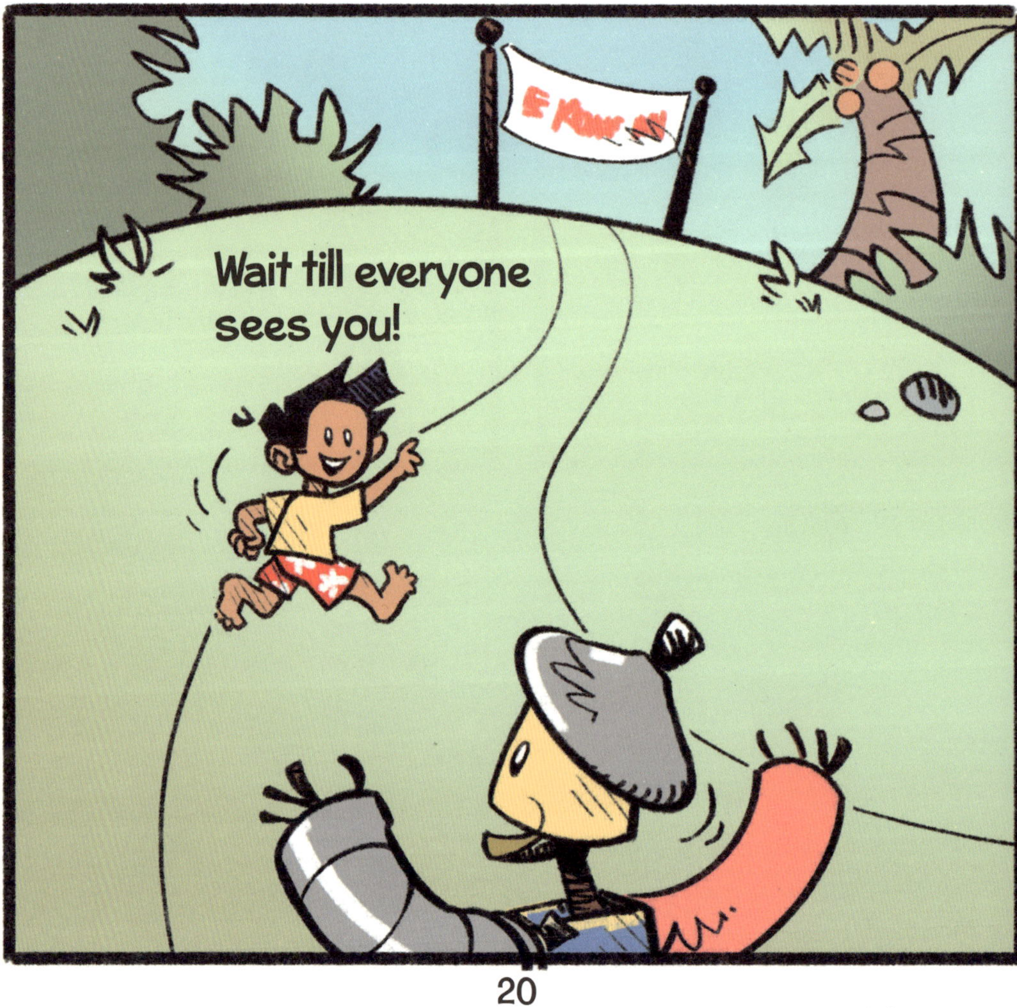
Wait till everyone
sees you!

chapter three

PARTY CRASHER

Haku and Sam arrive at a potluck welcoming Haku and his family to their new home.

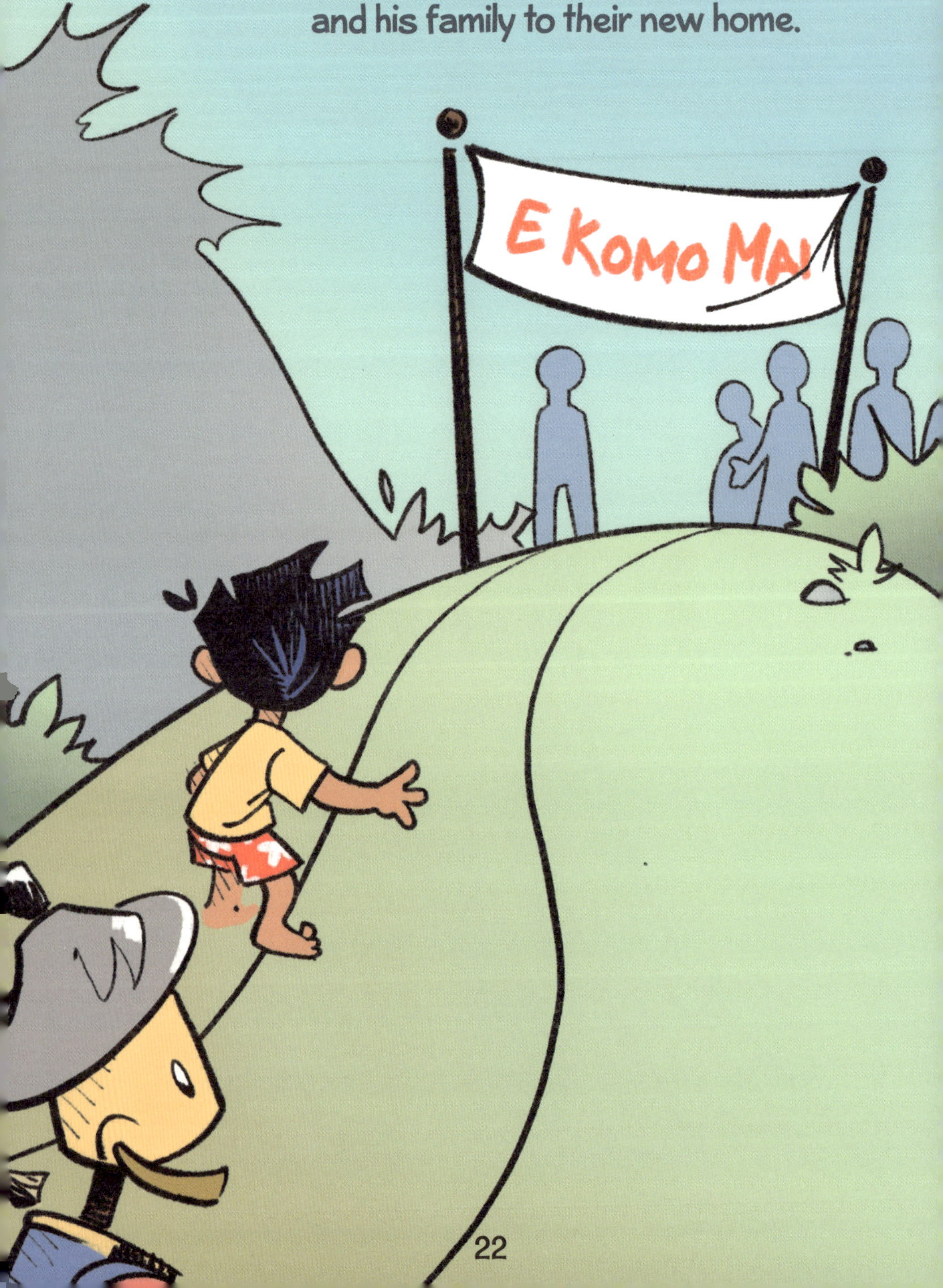
E KOMO MAI

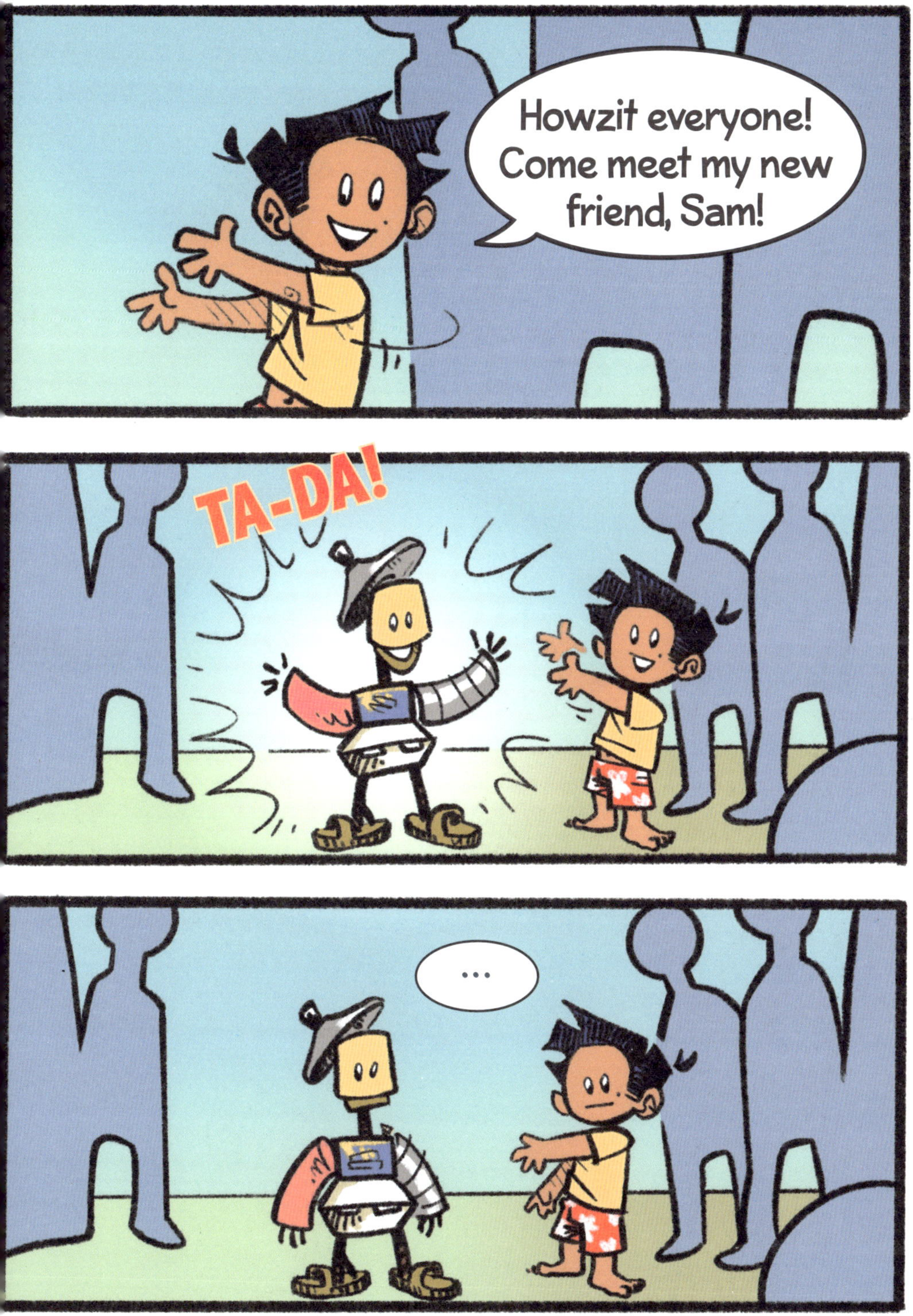
Howzit everyone! Come meet my new friend, Sam!
TA-DA!
...

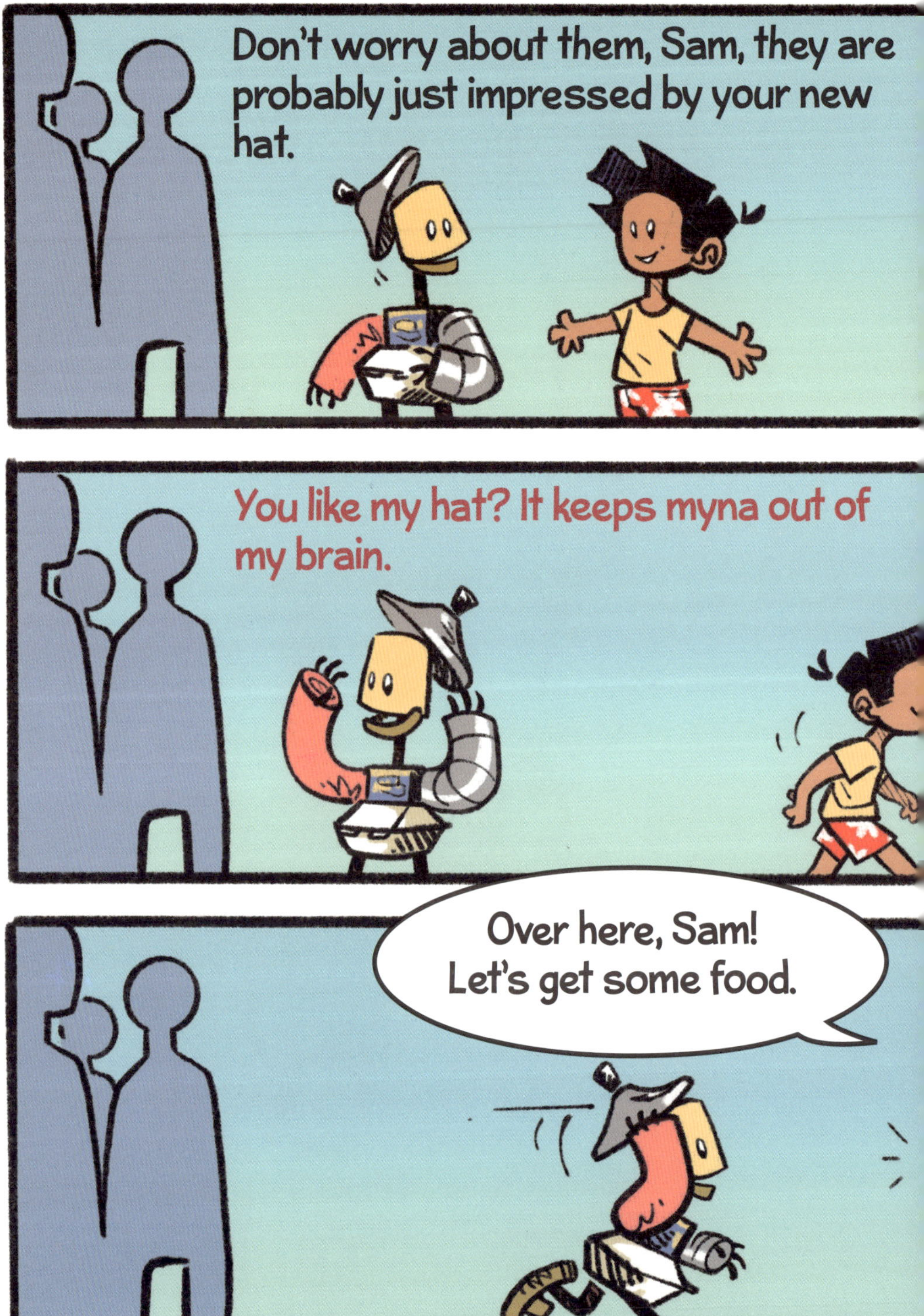
Don't worry about them, Sam, they are probably just impressed by your new hat.
You like my hat? It keeps myna out of my brain.
Over here, Sam! Let's get some food.

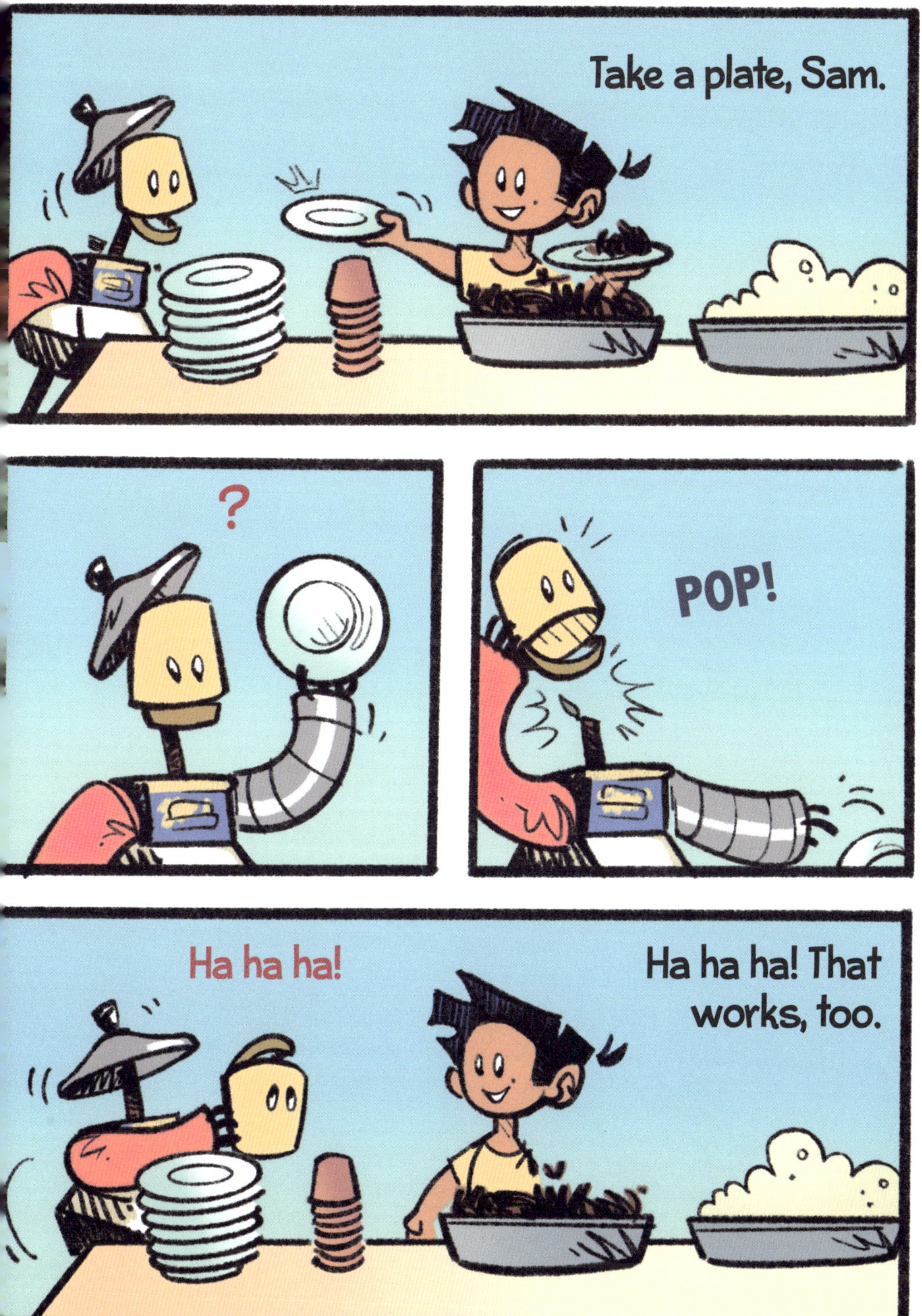
Take a plate, Sam.
?
POP!
Ha ha ha!
Ha ha ha! That works, too.

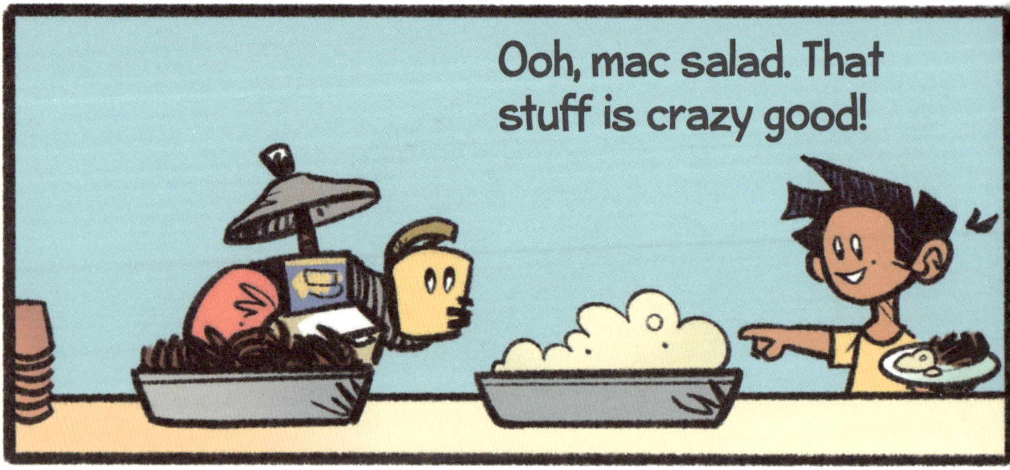
Ooh, mac salad. That stuff is crazy good!

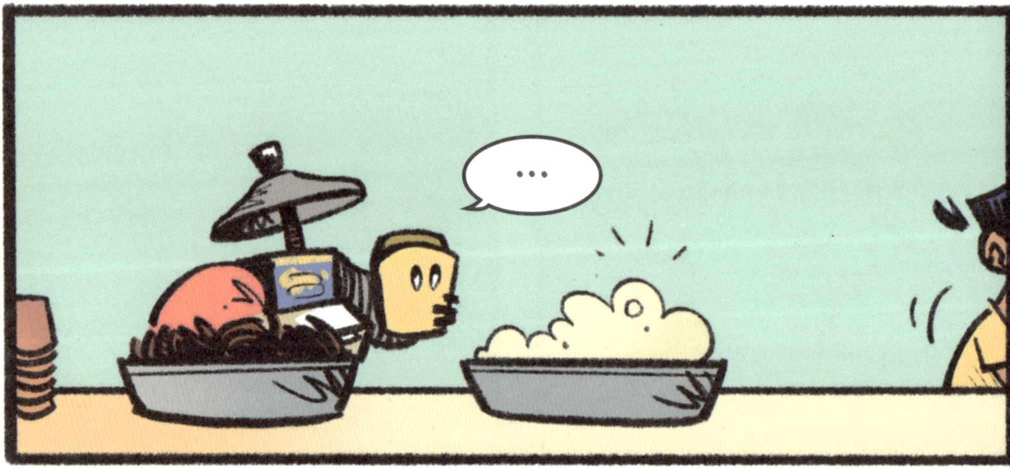
...

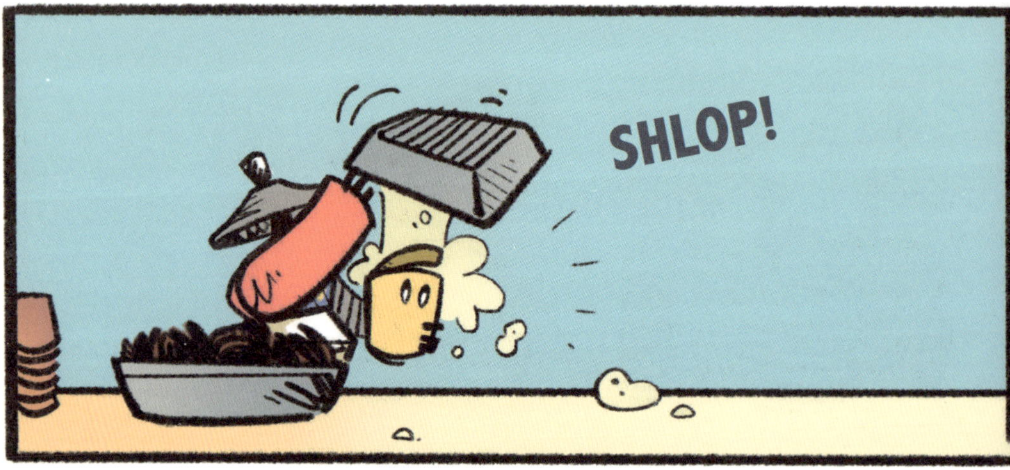
SHLOP!

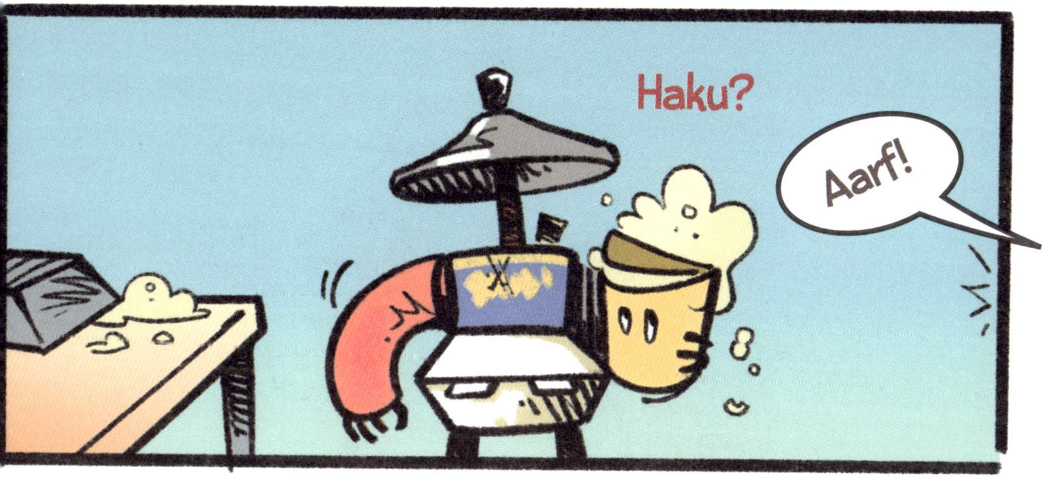
Haku?
Aarf!

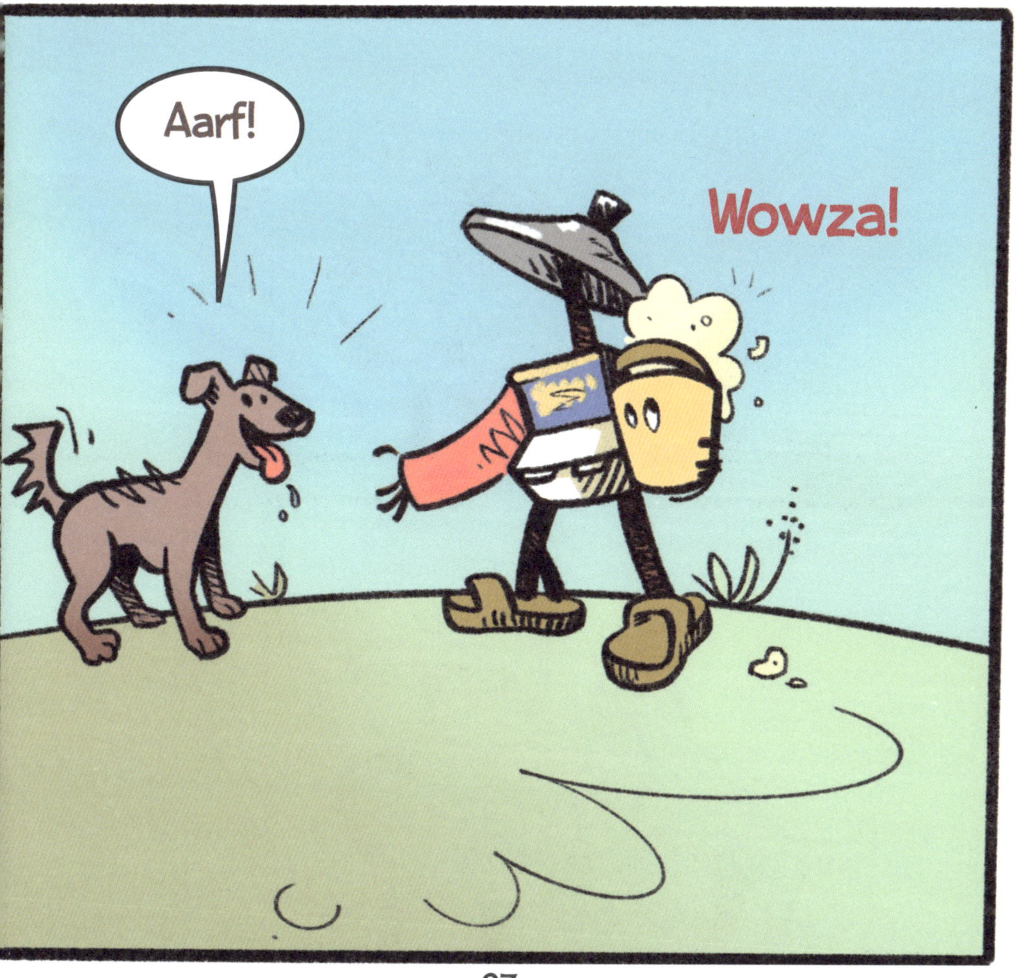
Aarf!
Wowza!

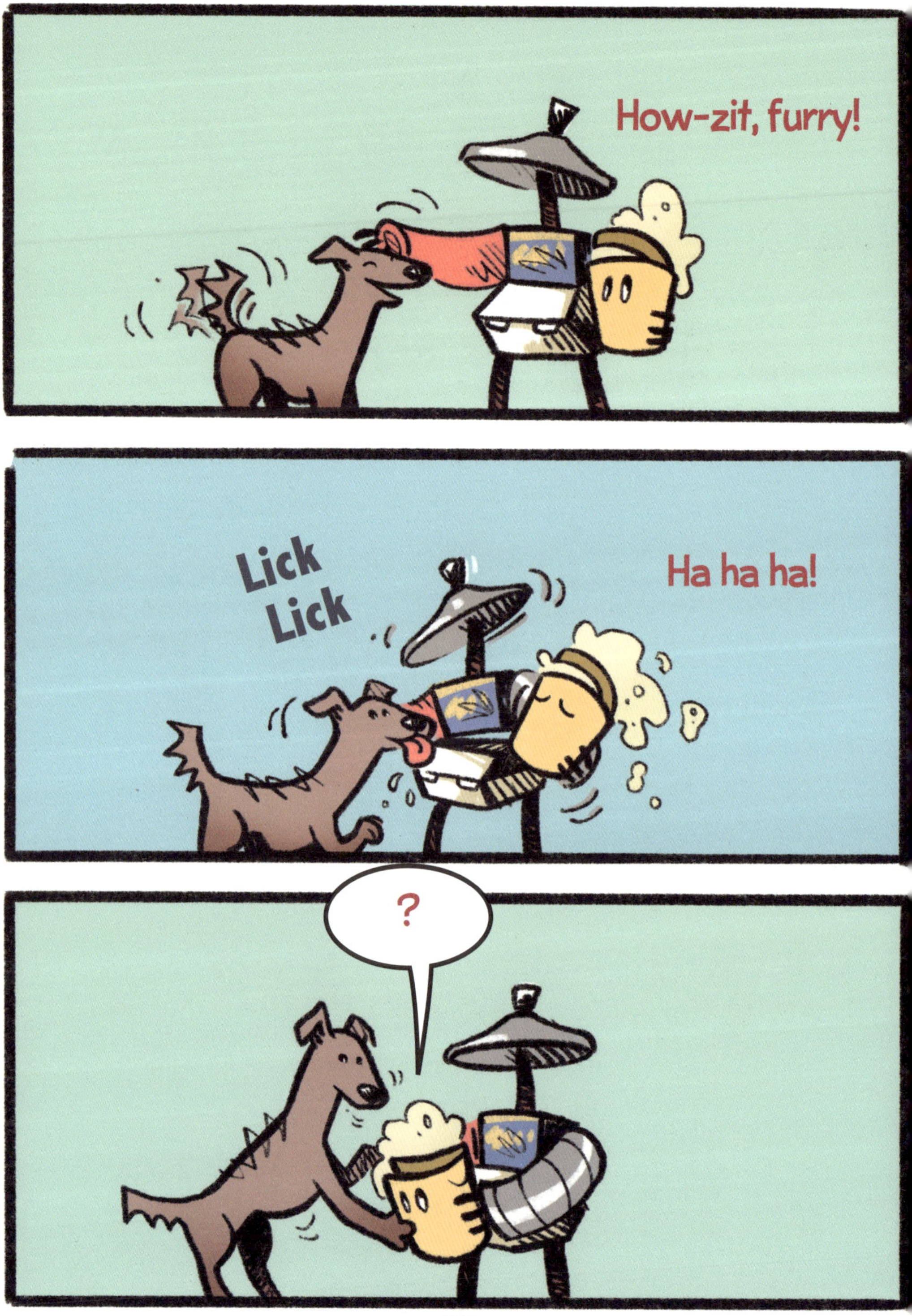
How-zit, furry!
Lick
Lick
Ha ha ha!
?

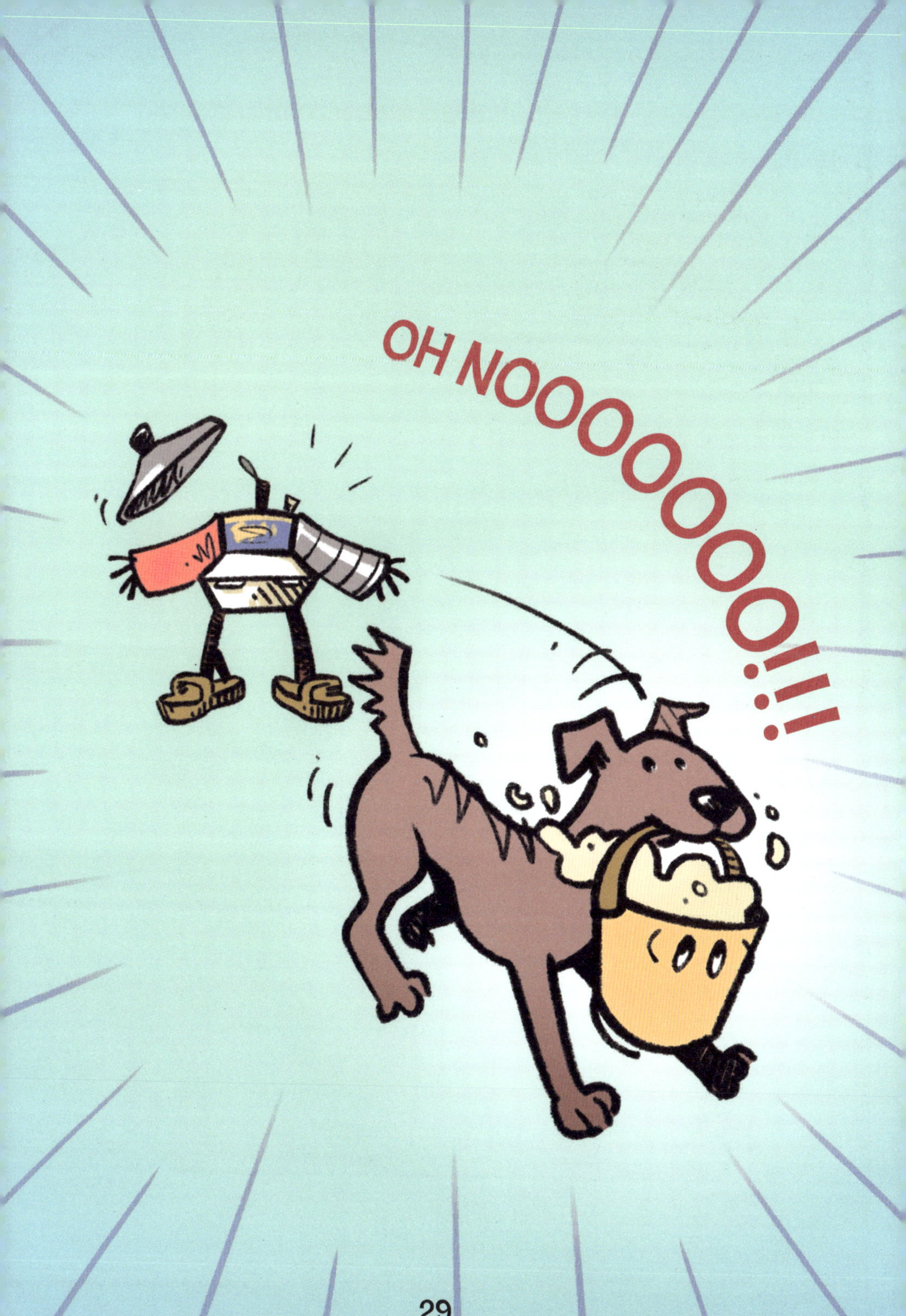
OH NOOOOOOOO!!!!

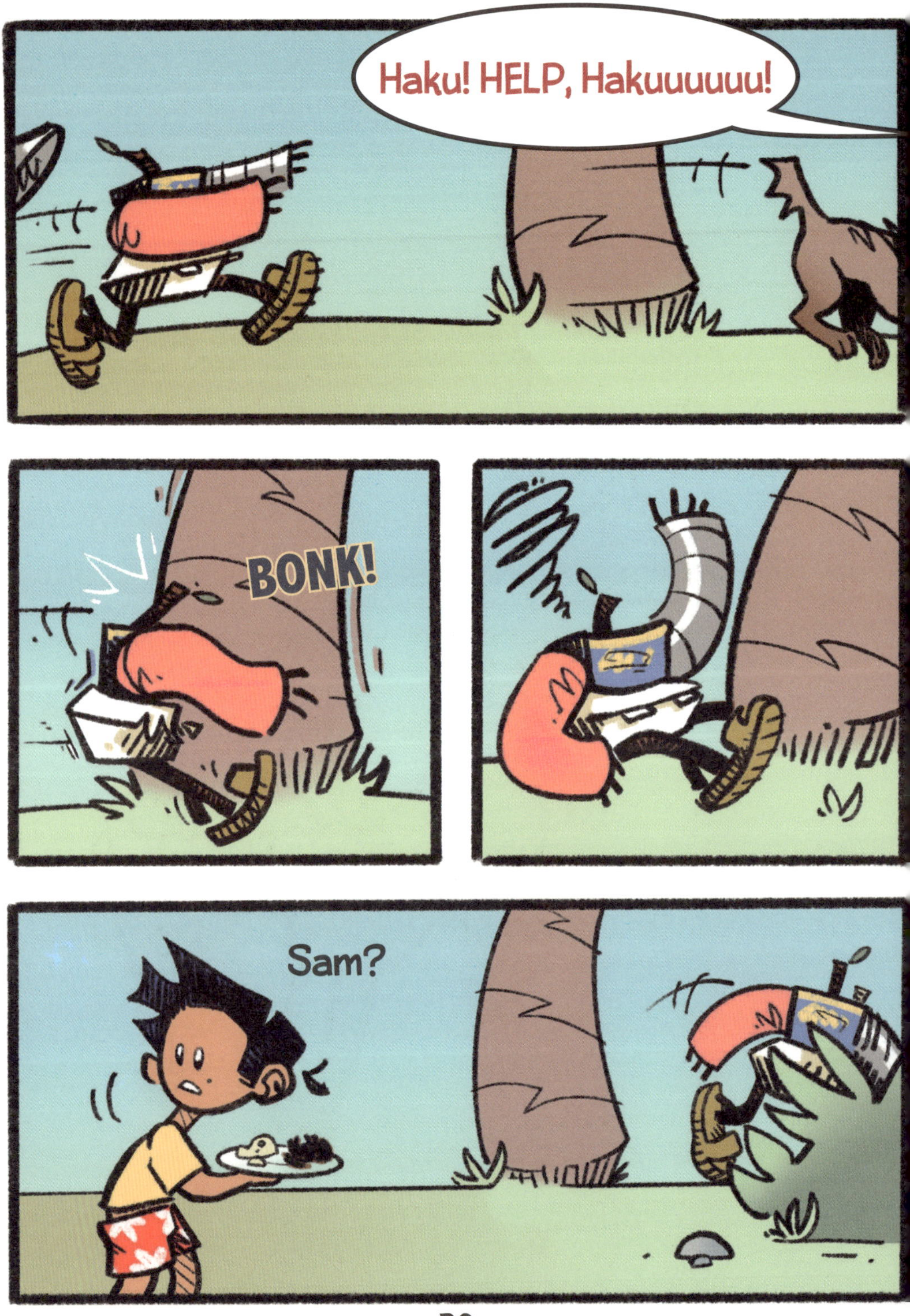
Haku! HELP, Hakuuuuuu!
BONK!
Sam?

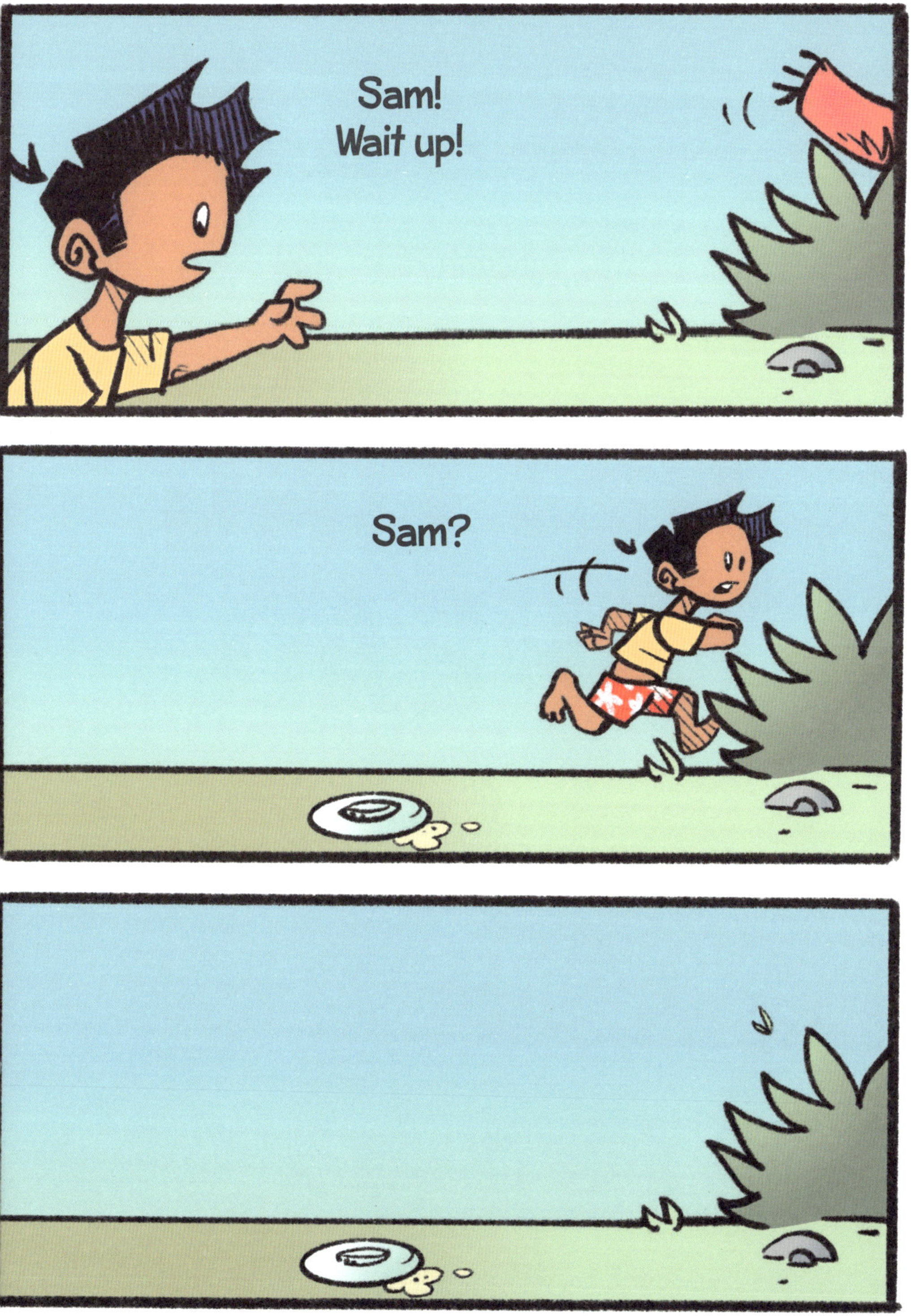
Sam!
Wait up!
Sam?

chapter four

GETTING AHEAD

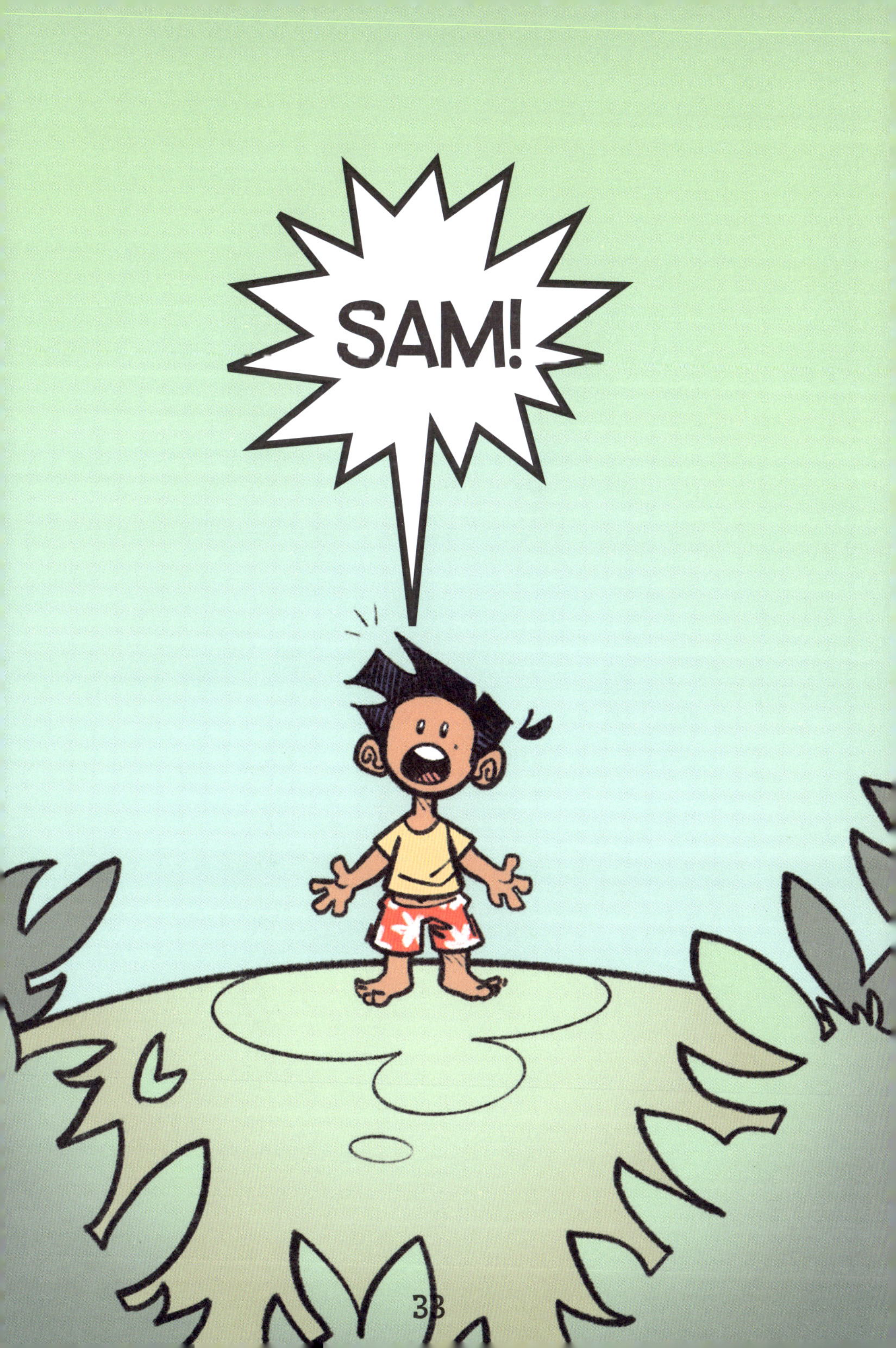
SAM!

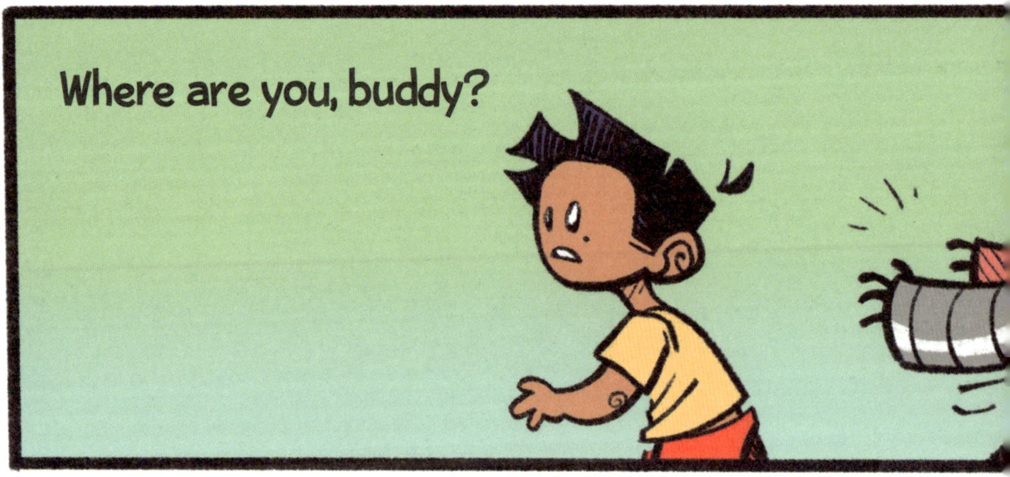
Where are you, buddy?

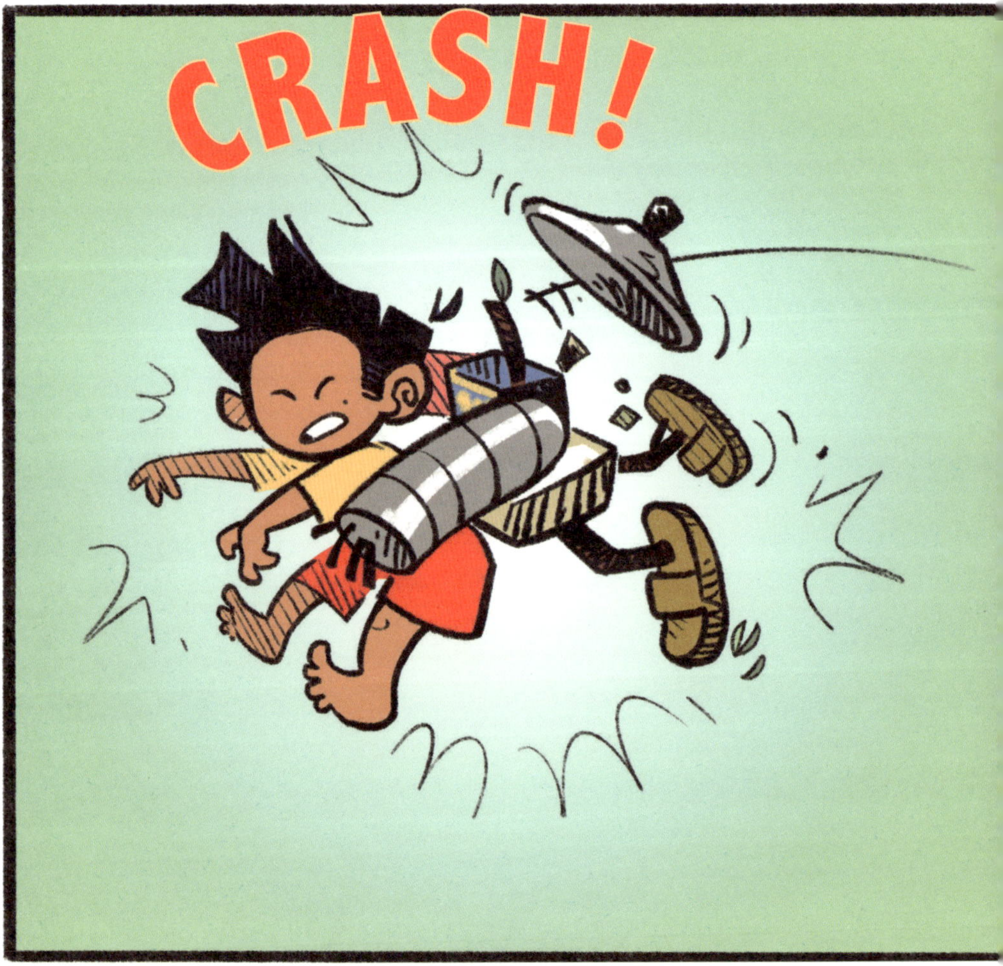
CRASH!

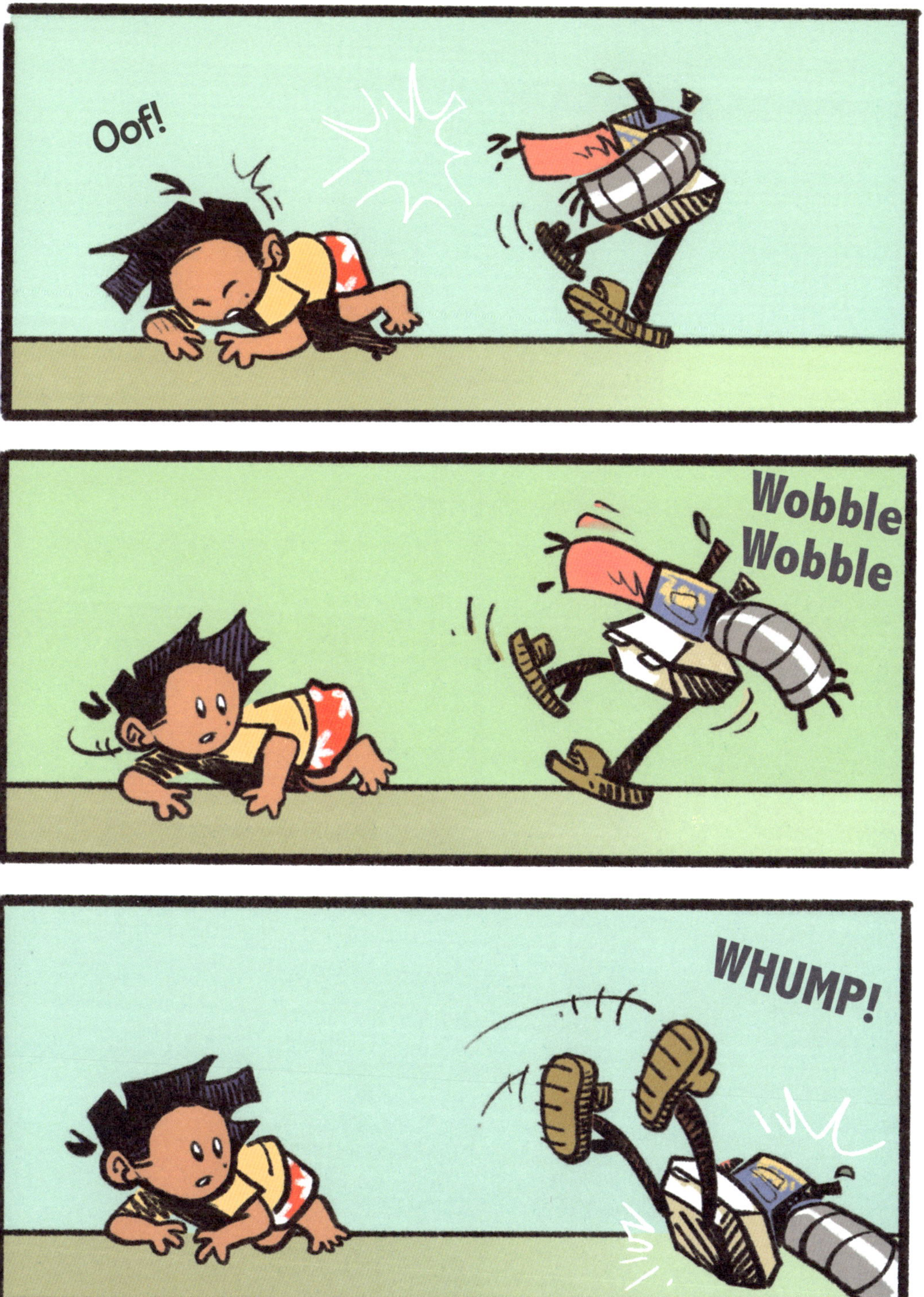
Oof!
Wobble
Wobble
WHUMP!

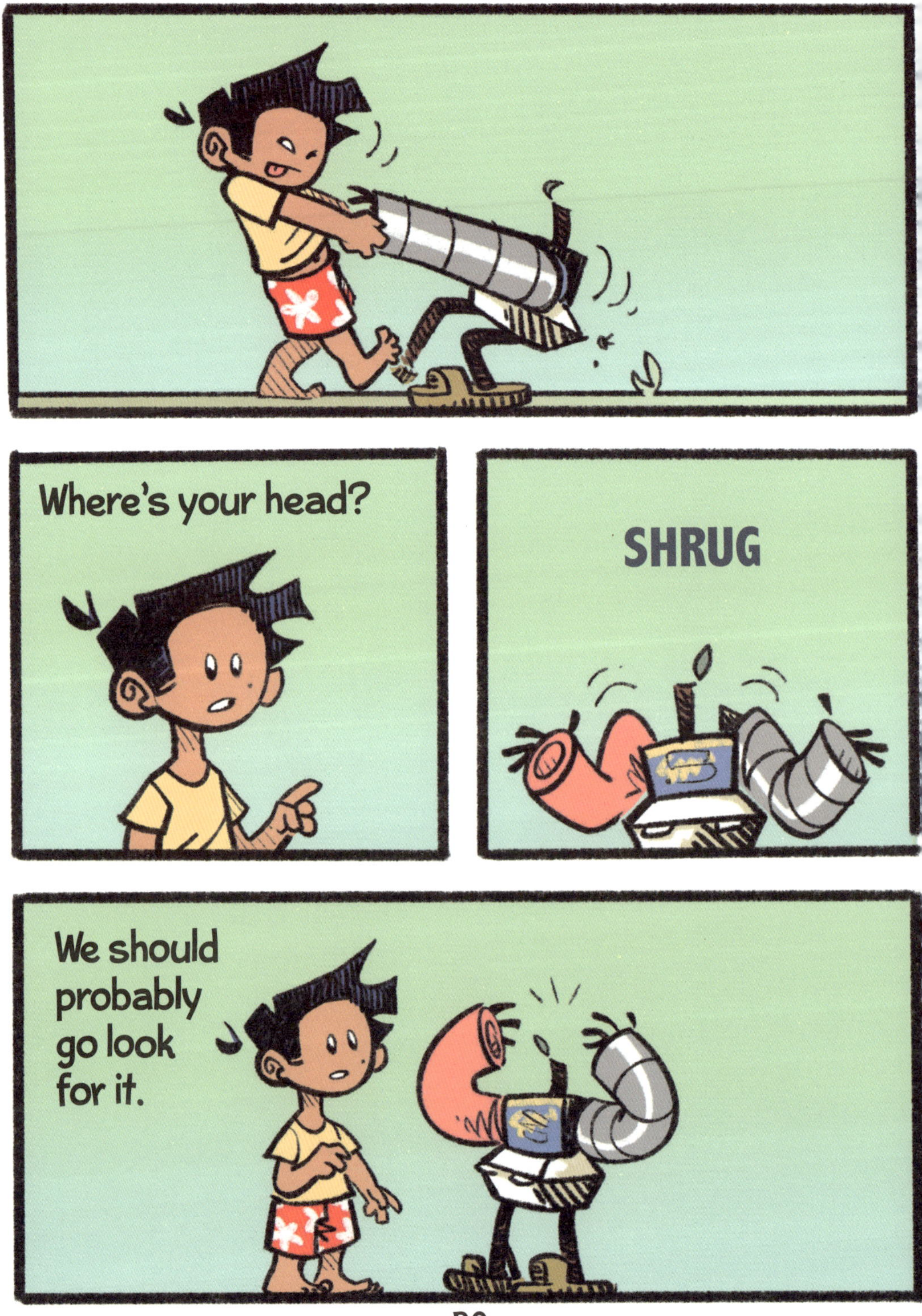
Where's your head?
SHRUG
We should probably go look for it.

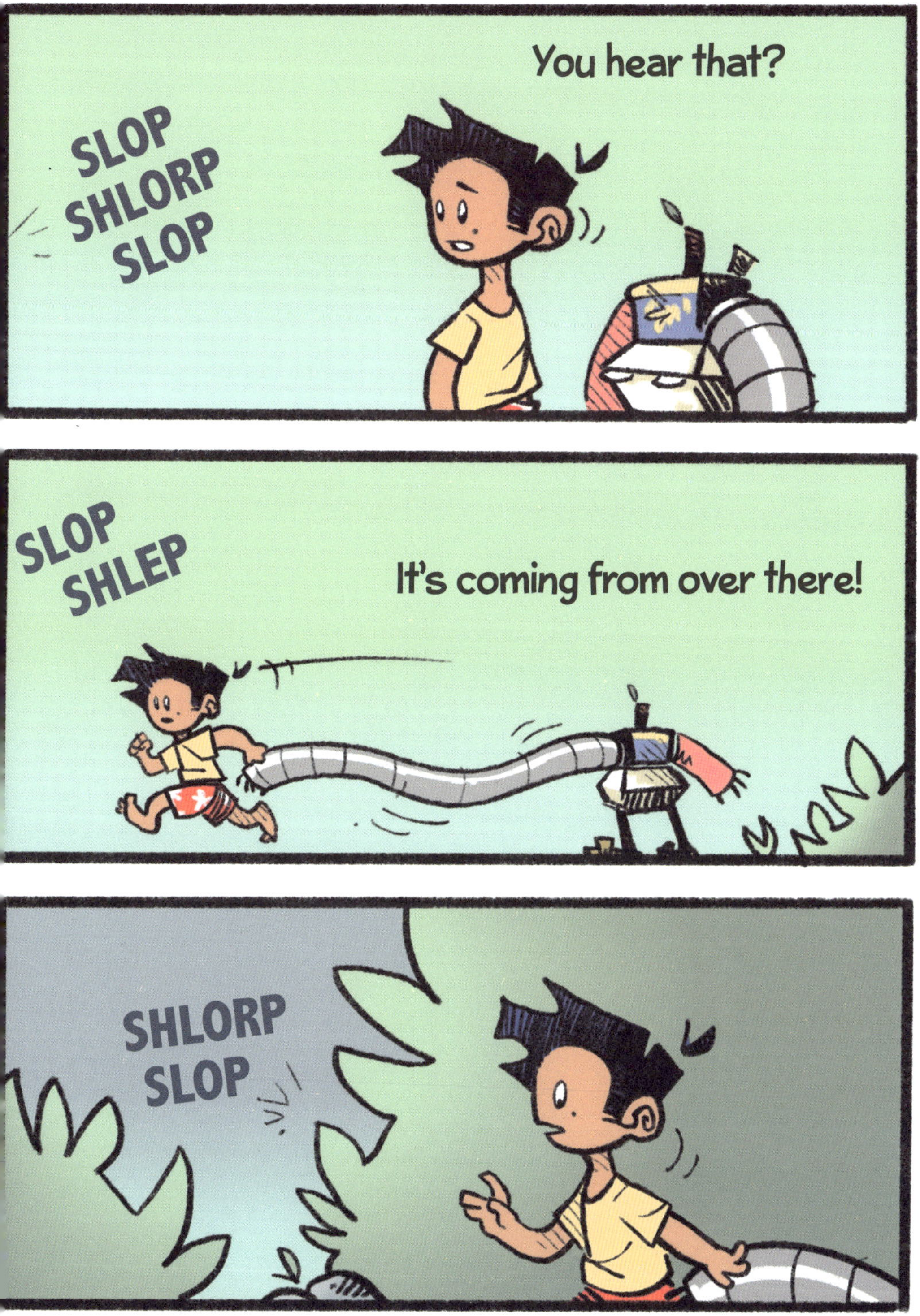
SLOP
SHLORP
SLOP
You hear that?
SLOP
SHLEP
It's coming from over there!
SHLORP
SLOP

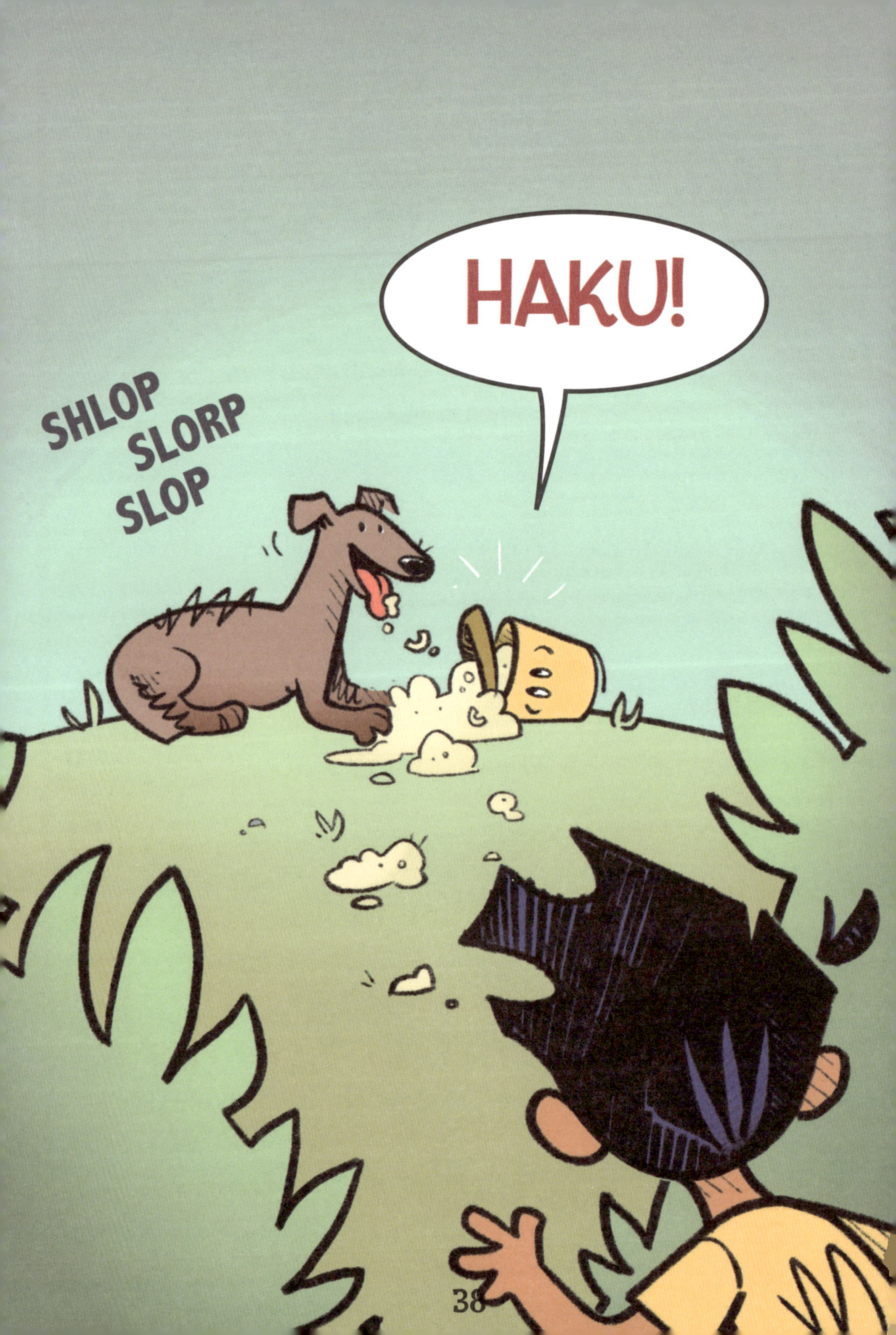
SHLOP
SLORP
SLOP
HAKU!

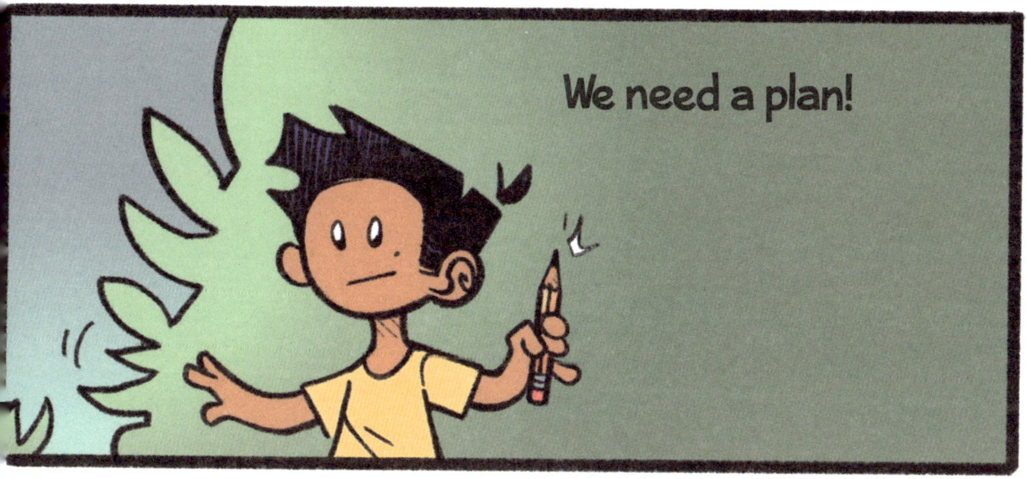
We need a plan!

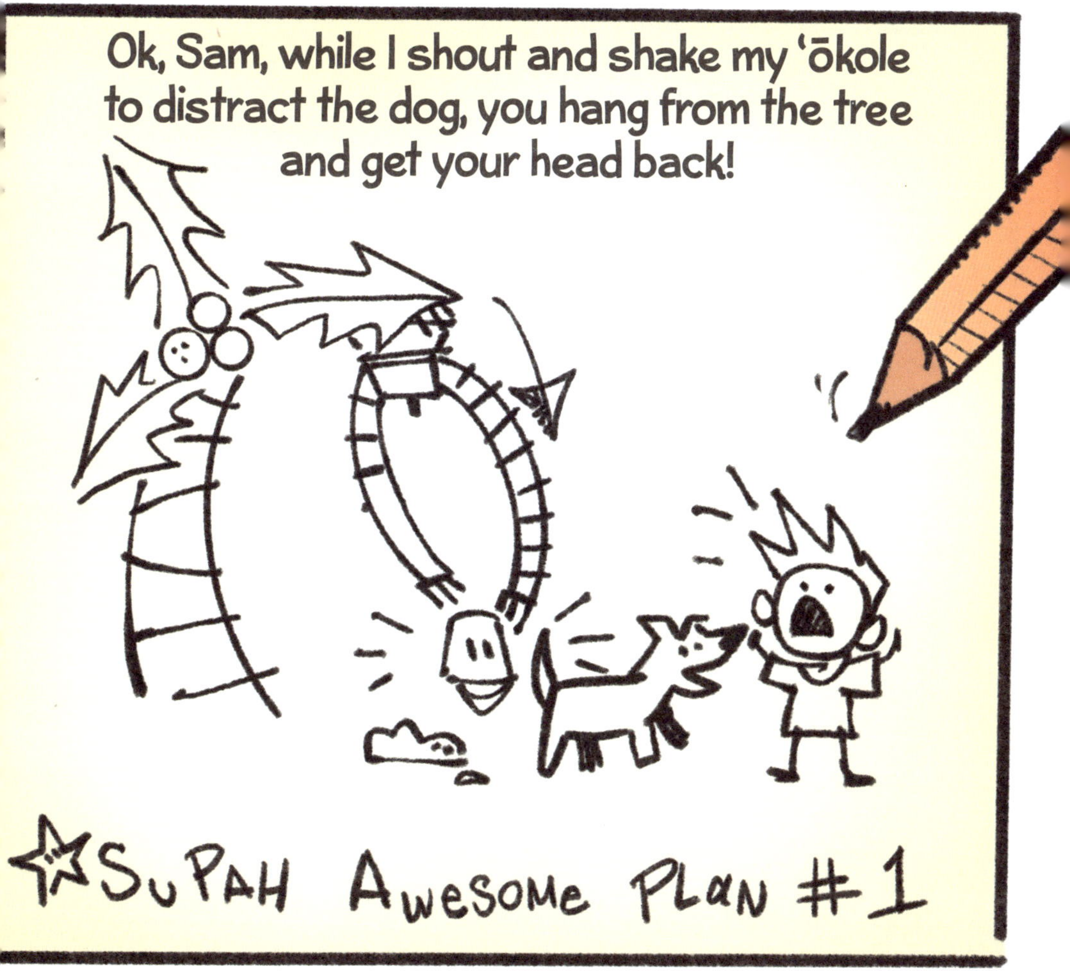
Ok, Sam, while I shout and shake my ʻōkole to distract the dog, you hang from the tree and get your head back!
SUPAH AWESOME PLAN #1

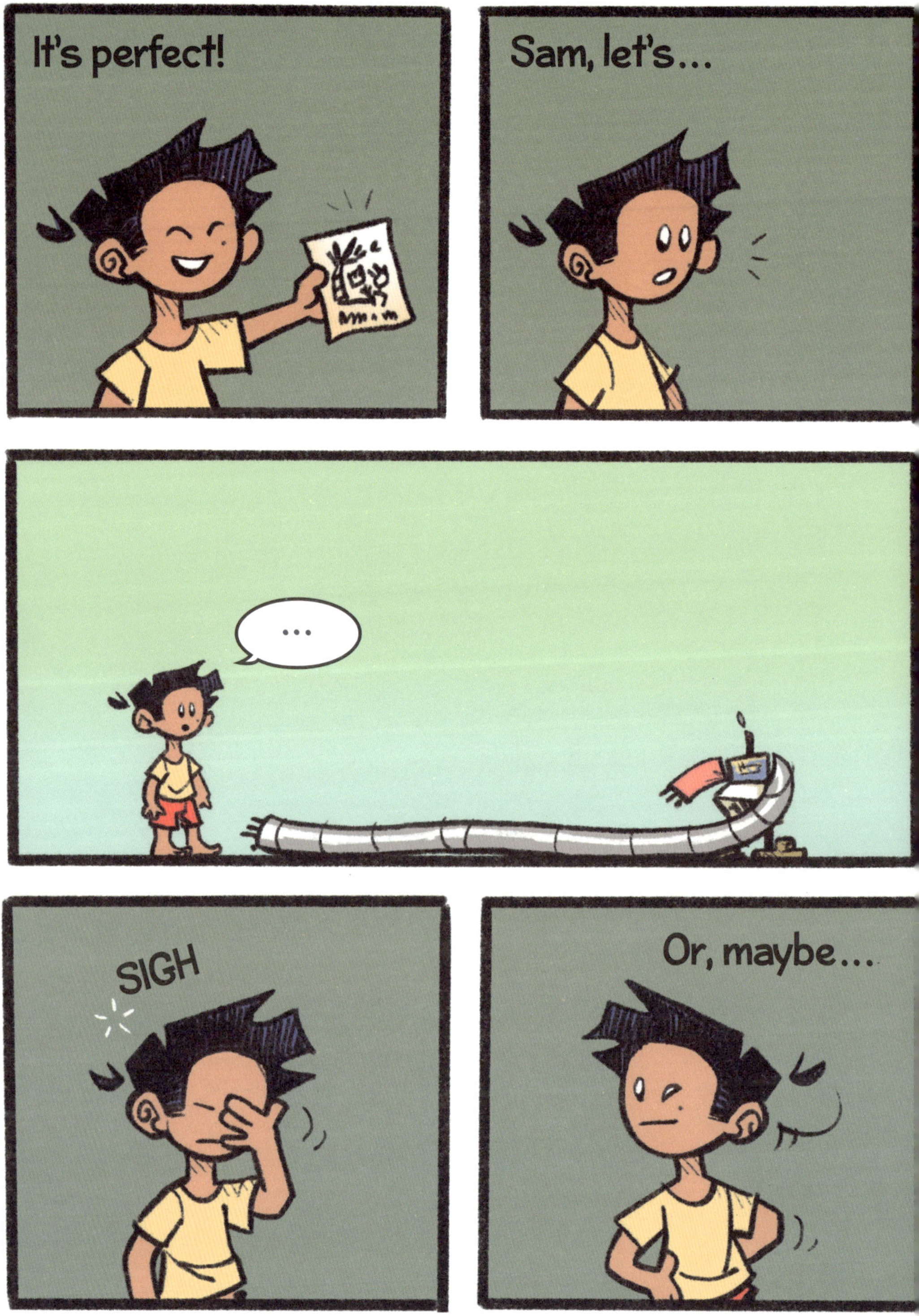
It's perfect!
Sam, let's...
...
SIGH
Or, maybe...

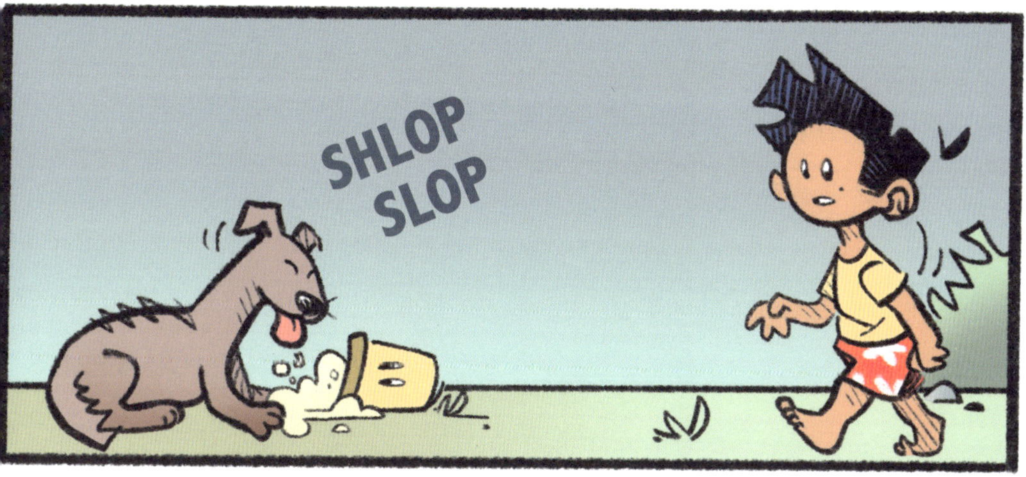
SHLOP
SLOP

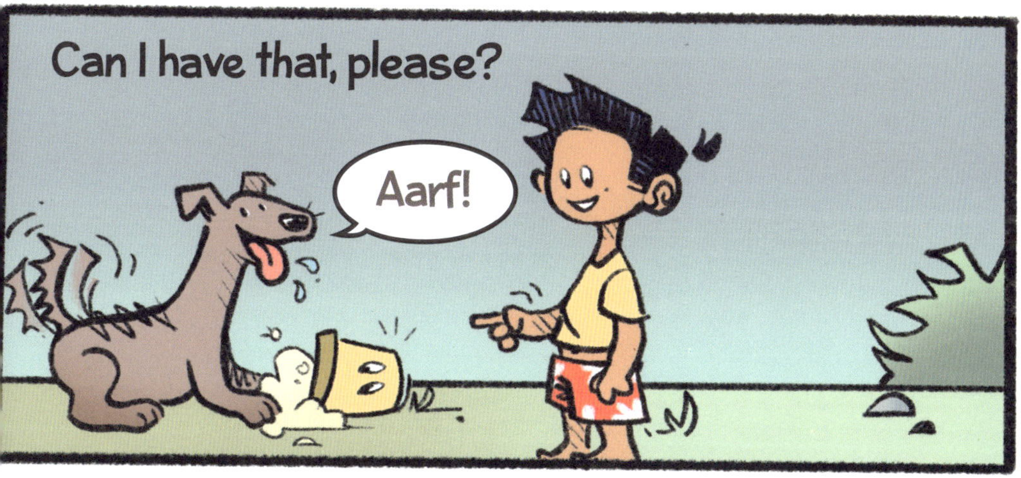
Can I have that, please?
Aarf!

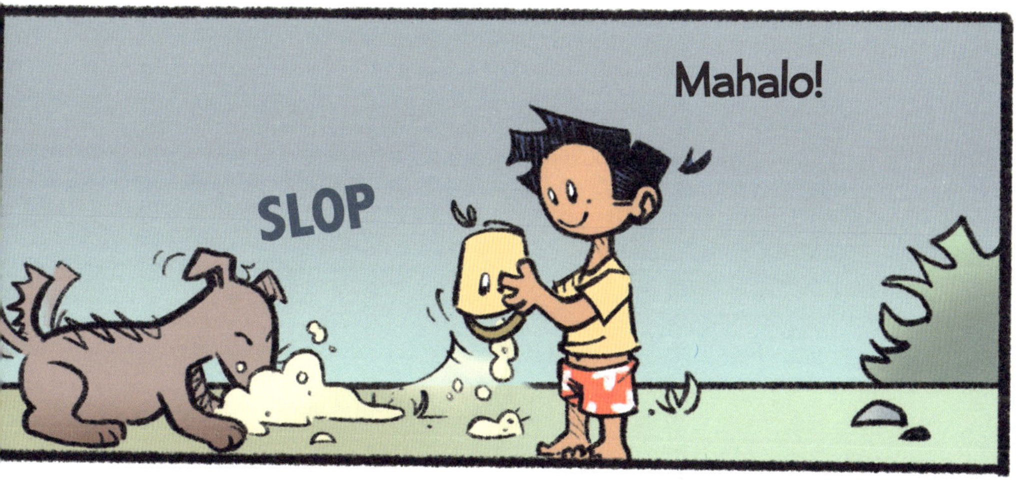
Mahalo!
SLOP

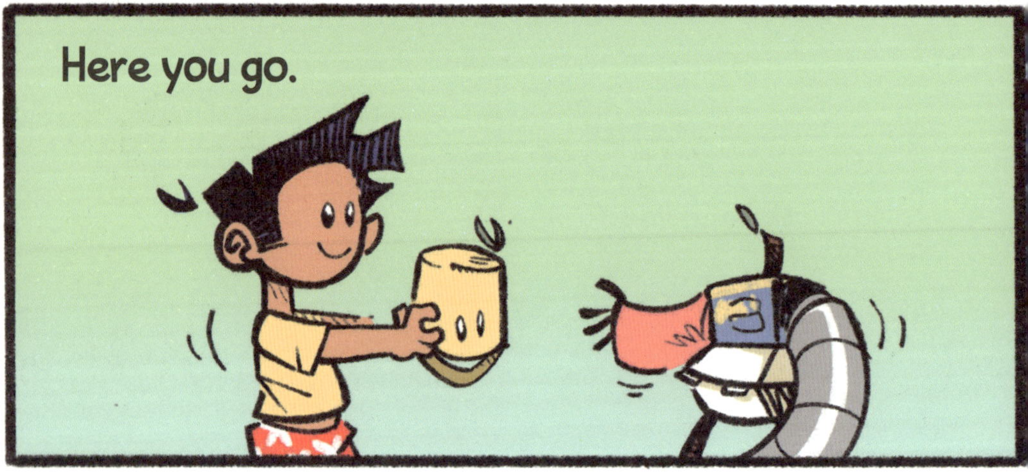
Here you go.

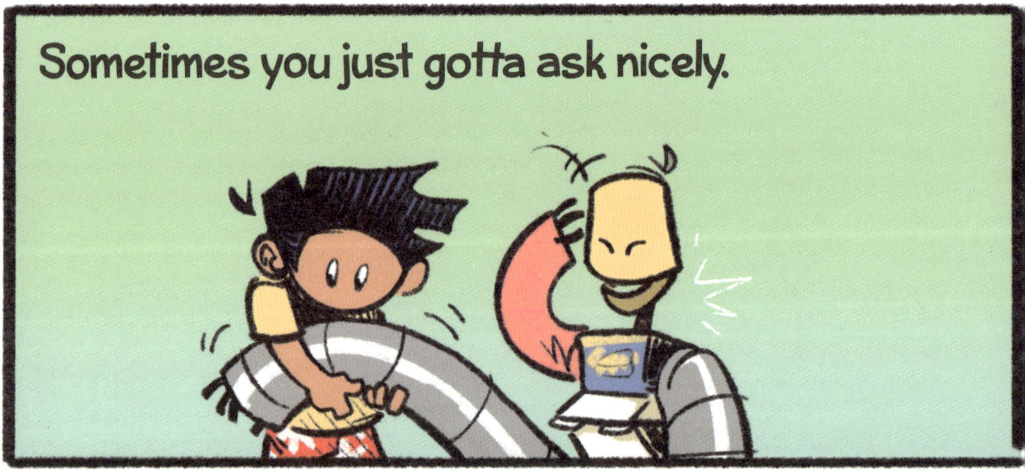
Sometimes you just gotta ask nicely.

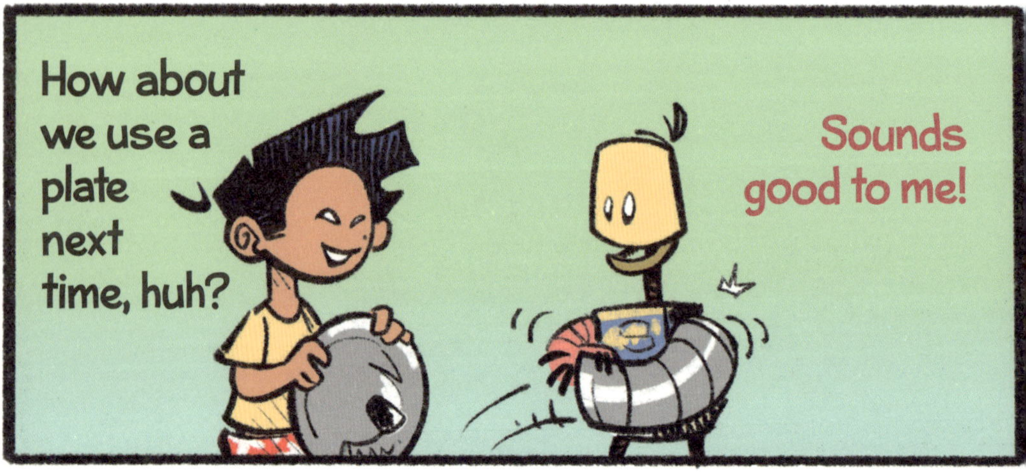
How about we use a plate next time, huh?
Sounds good to me!

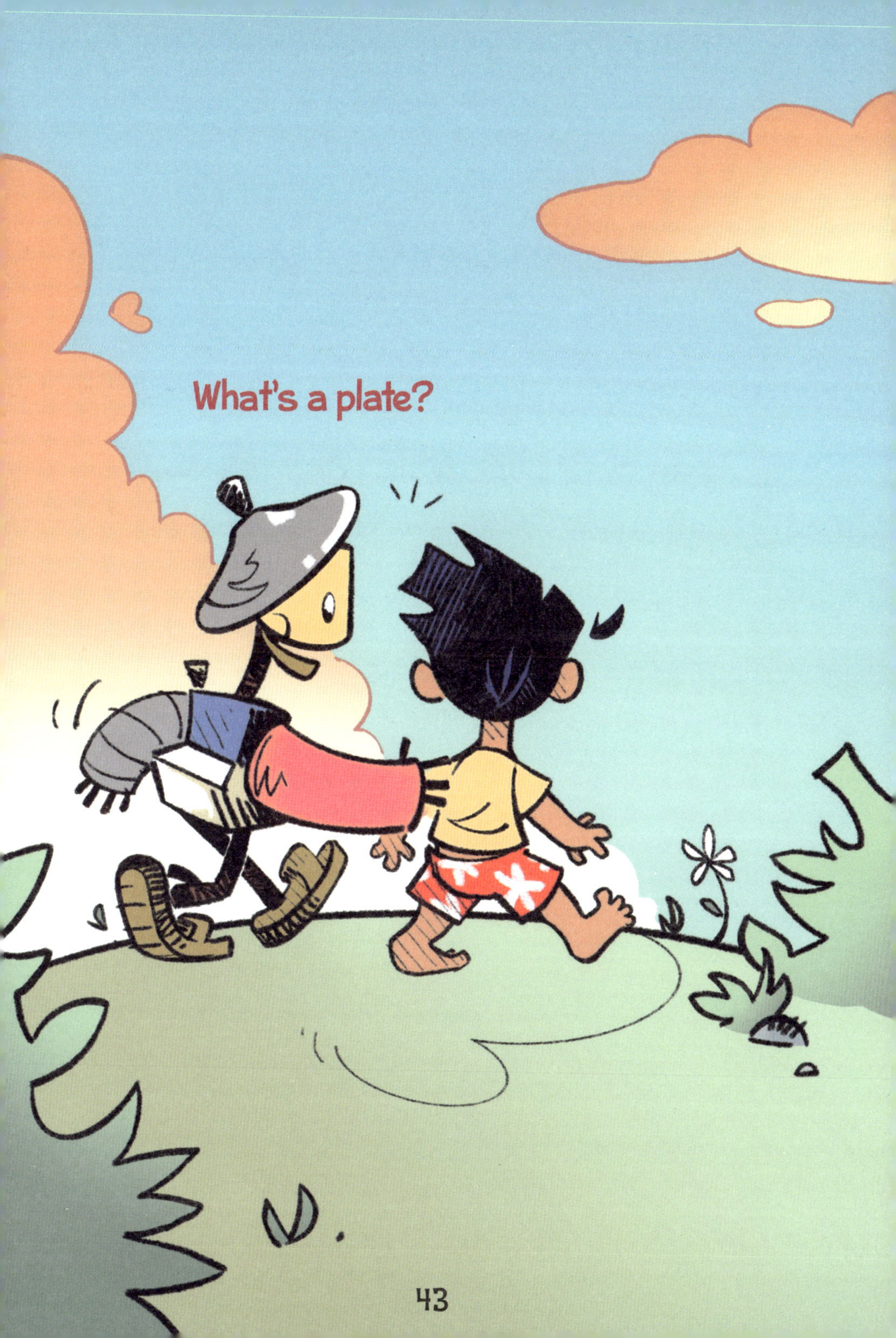
What's a plate?

chapter five

UNPACKING

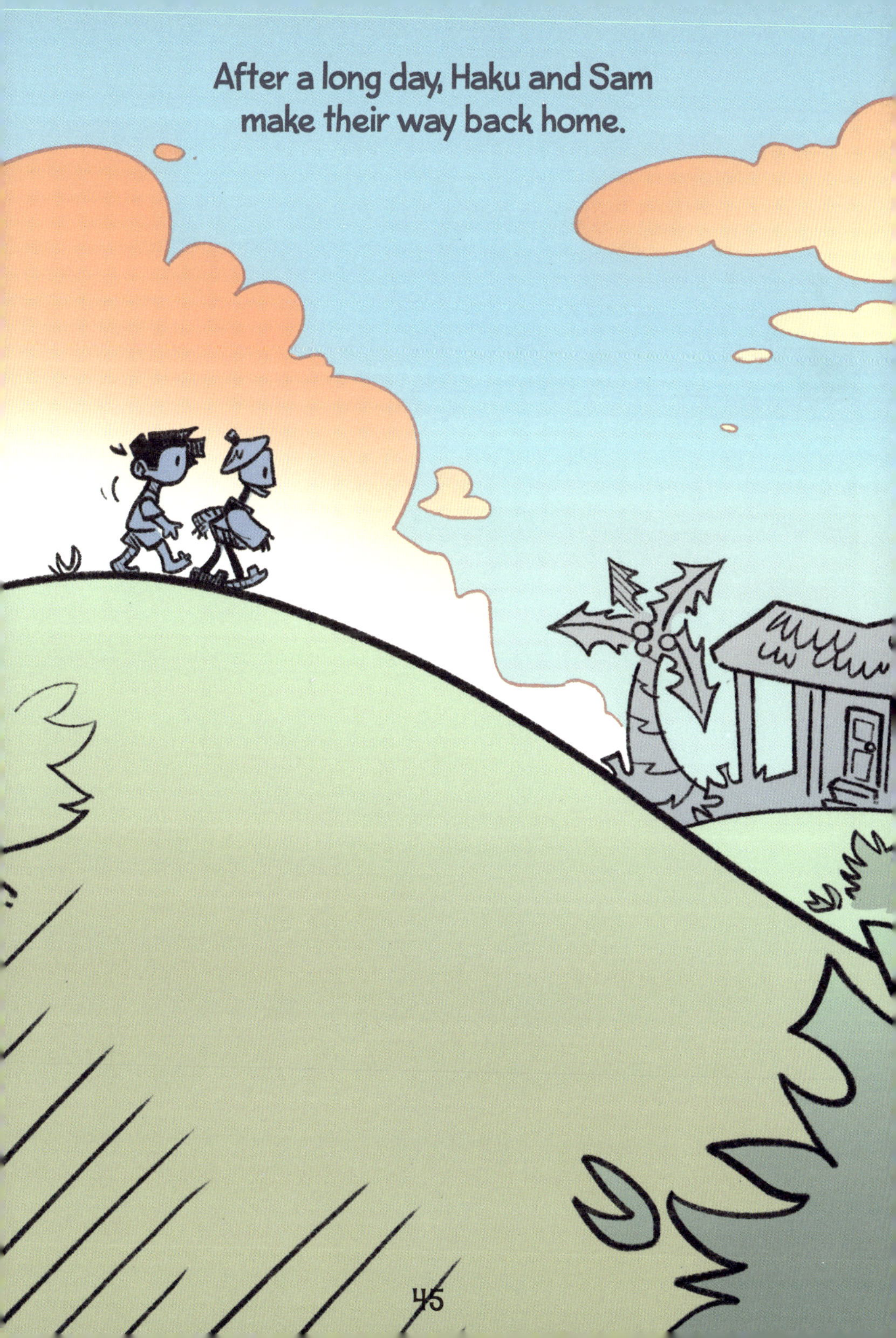
After a long day, Haku and Sam make their way back home.

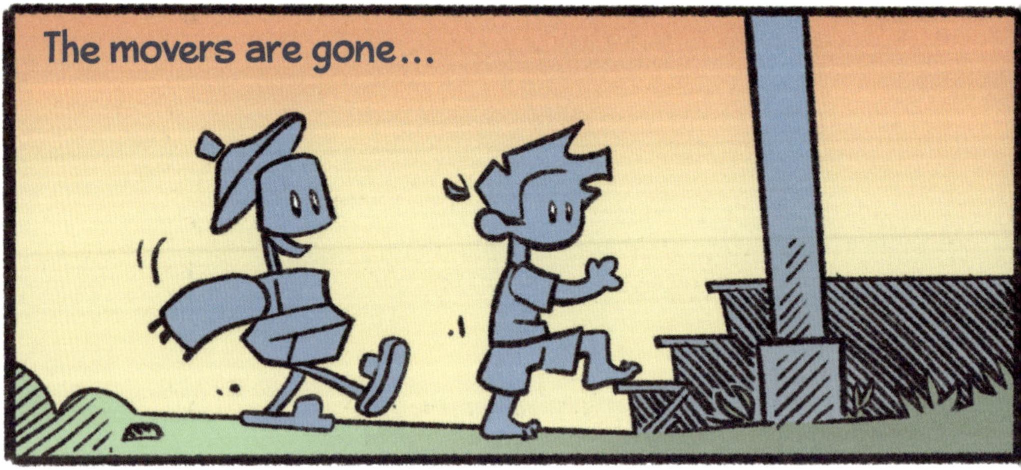
The movers are gone...

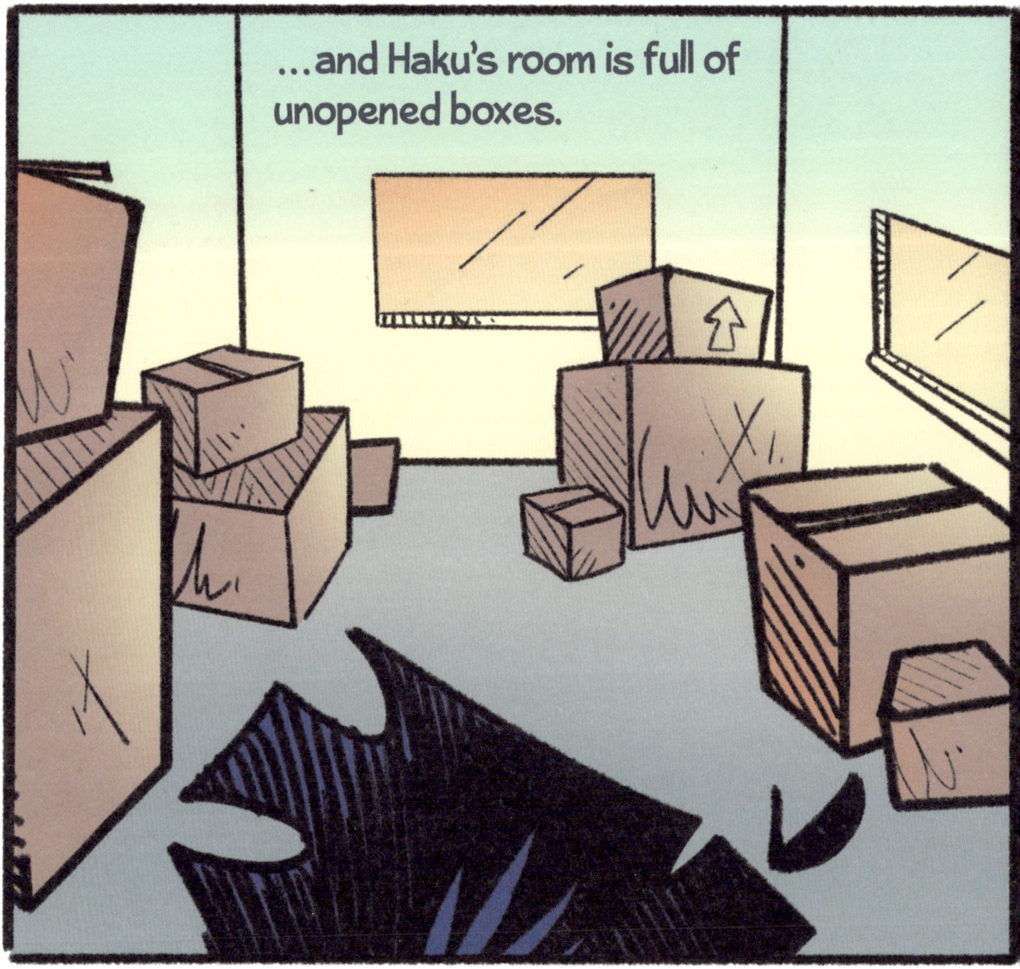
...and Haku's room is full of
unopened boxes.

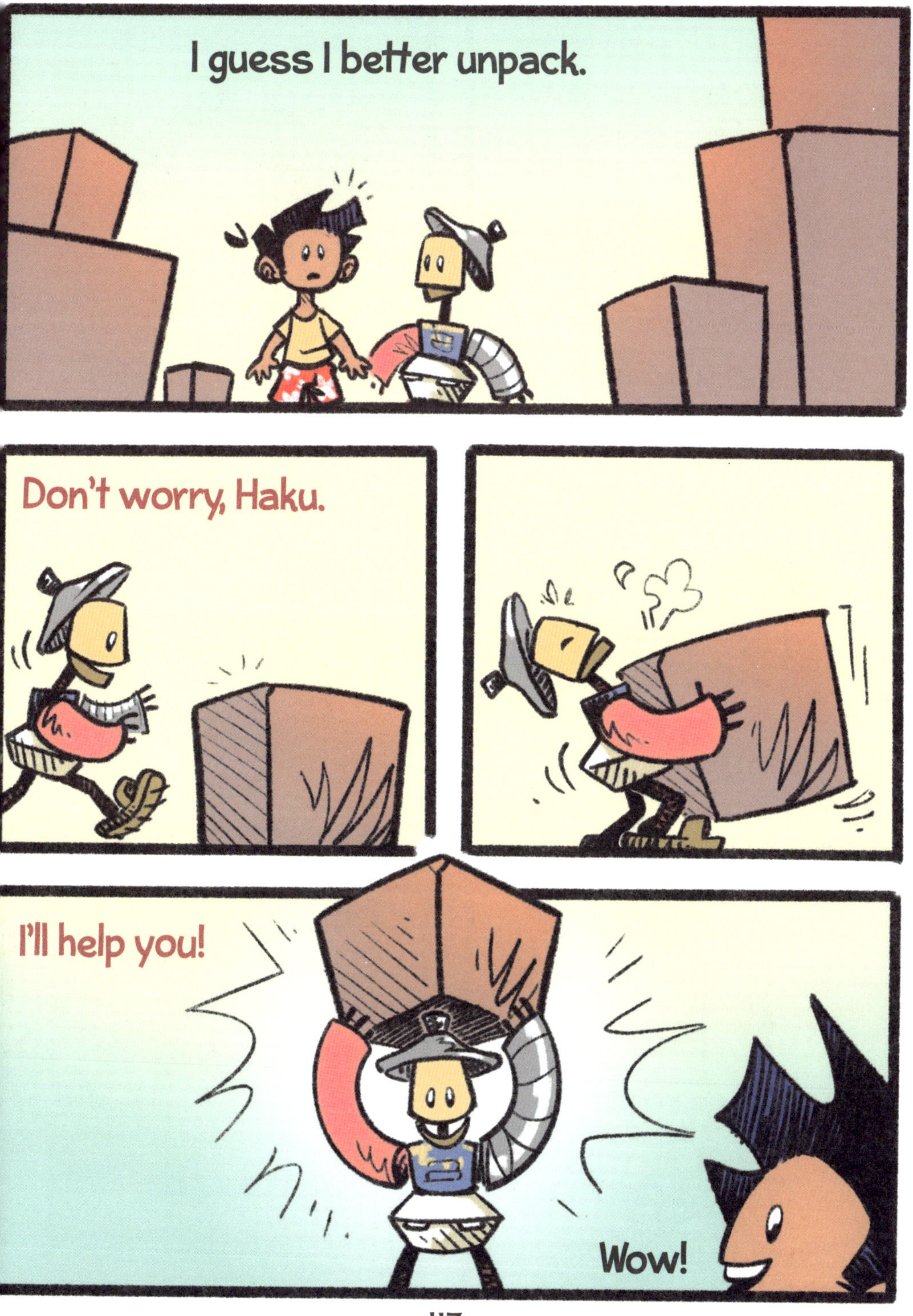
I guess I better unpack.
Don't worry, Haku.
I'll help you!
Wow!

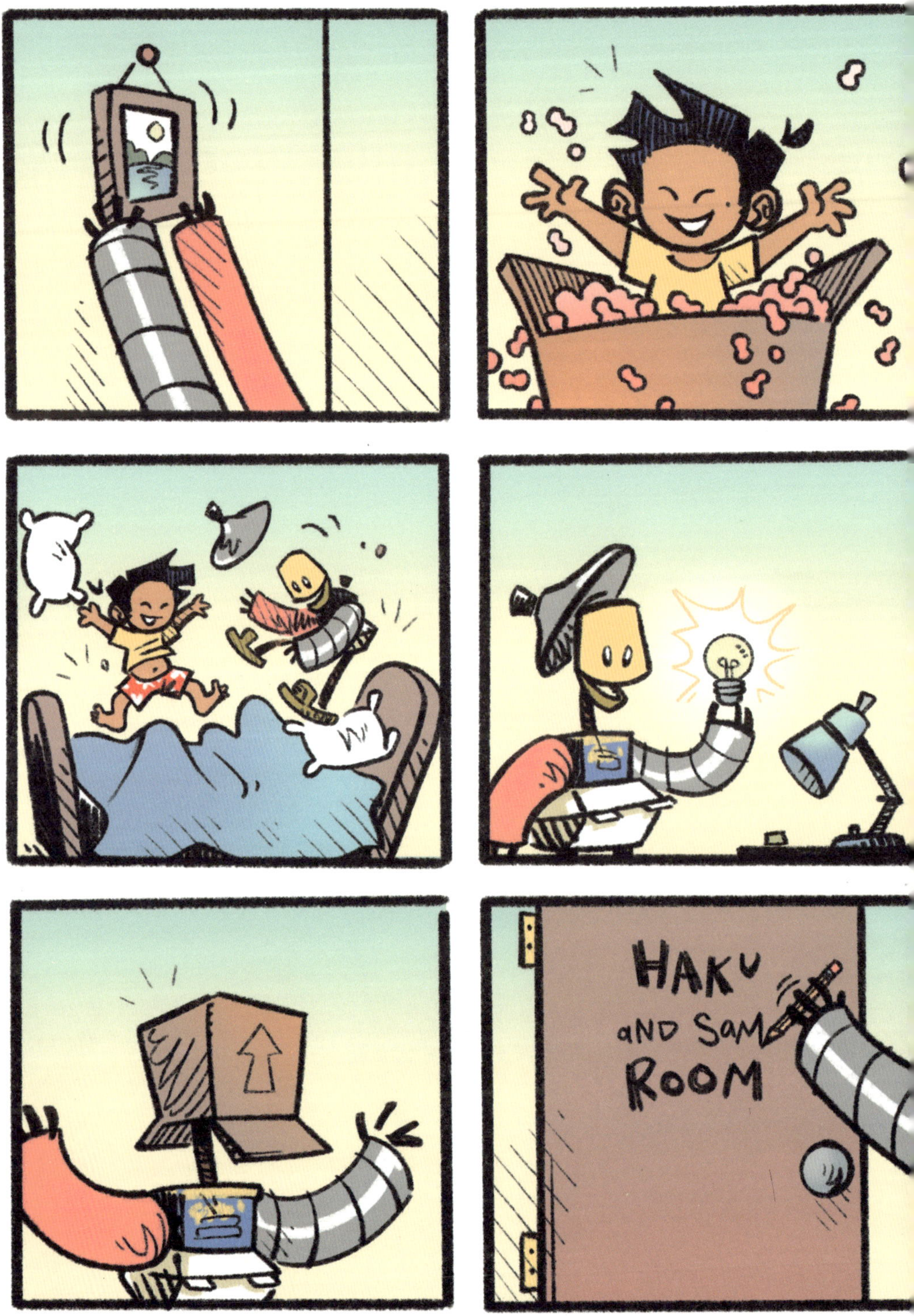
HAKU
AND SAM
ROOM

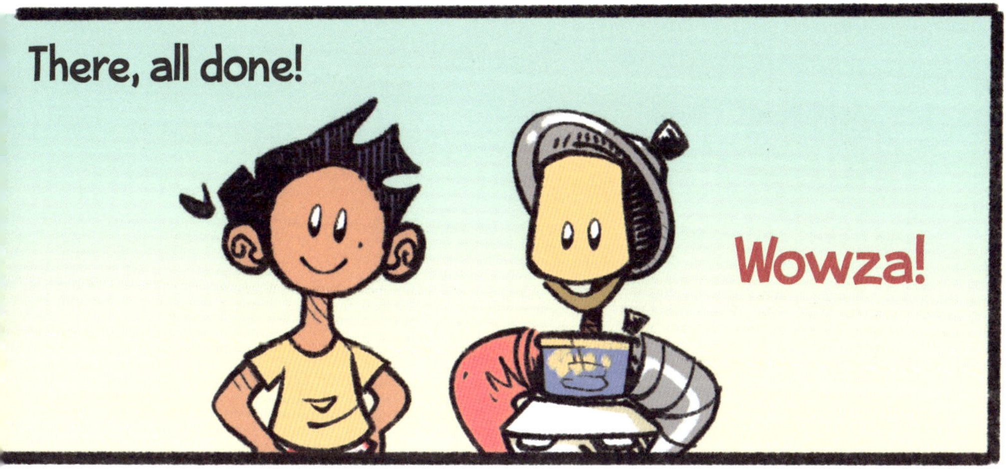
There, all done!
Wowza!

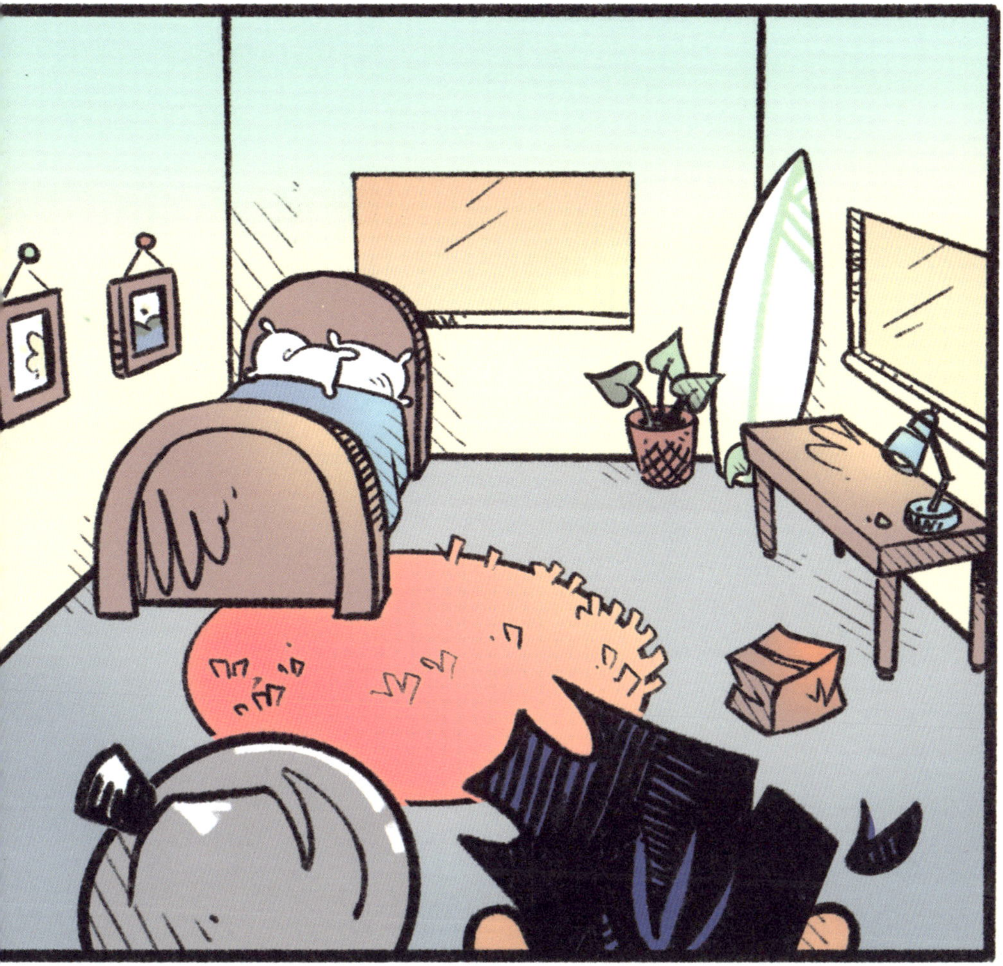

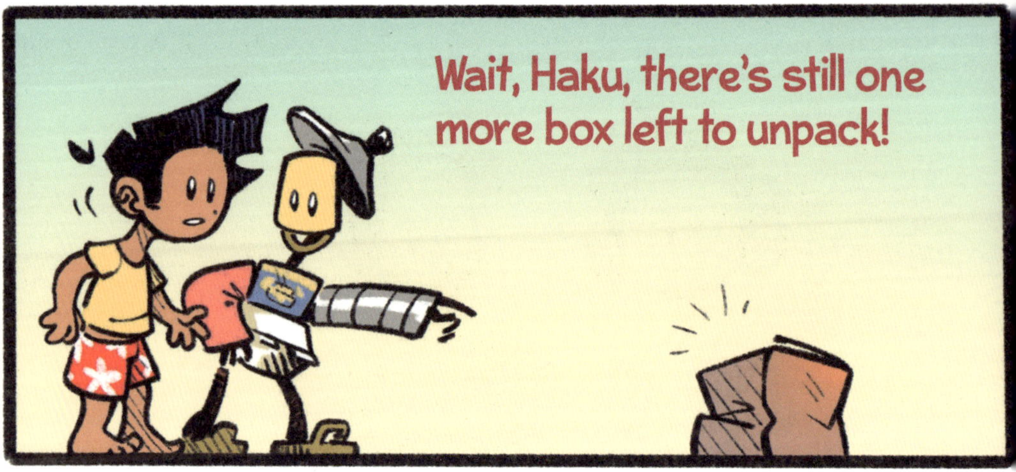
Wait, Haku, there's still one more box left to unpack!

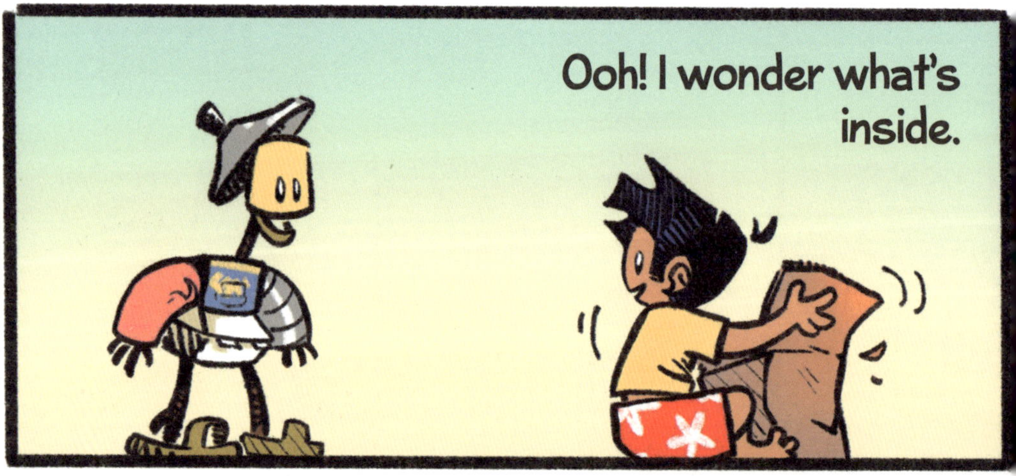
Ooh! I wonder what's inside.

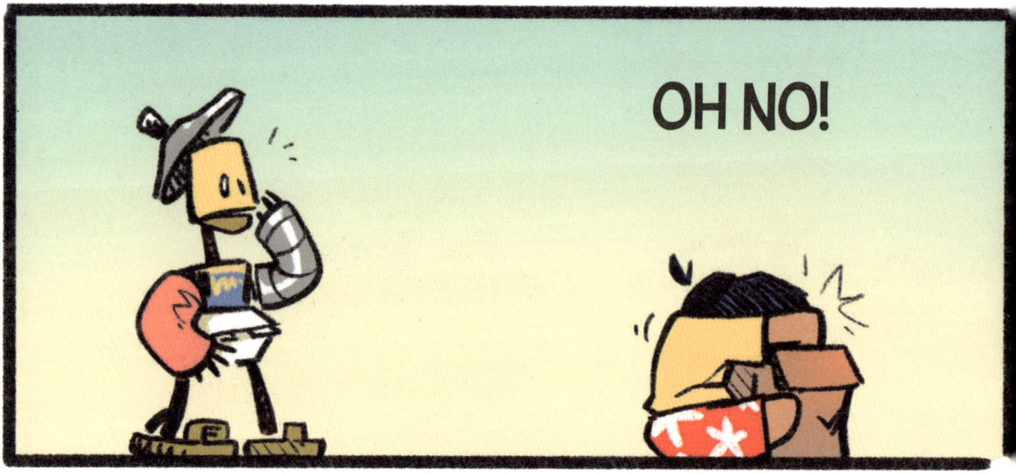
OH NO!

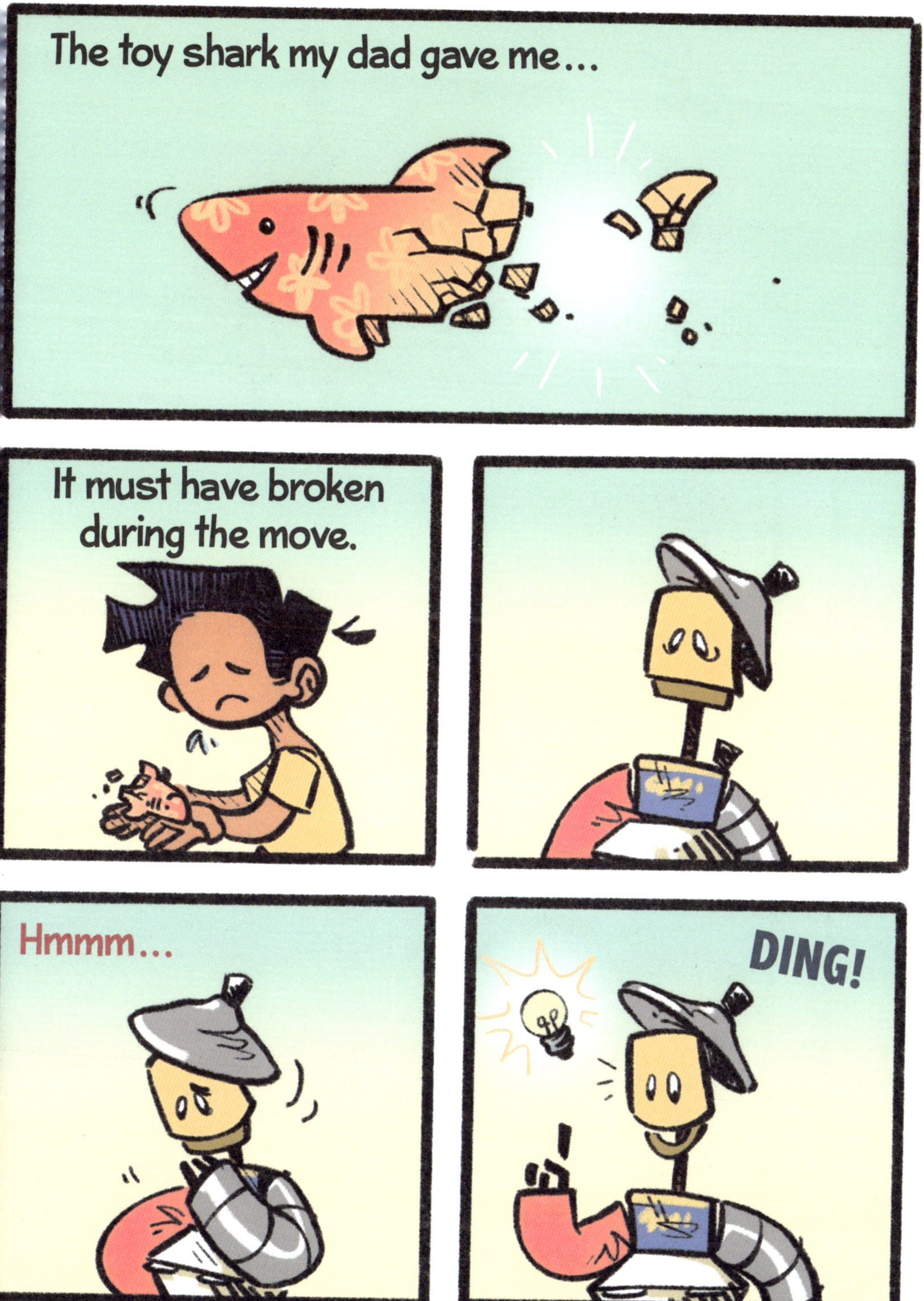
The toy shark my dad gave me...
It must have broken during the move.
Hmmm...
DING!

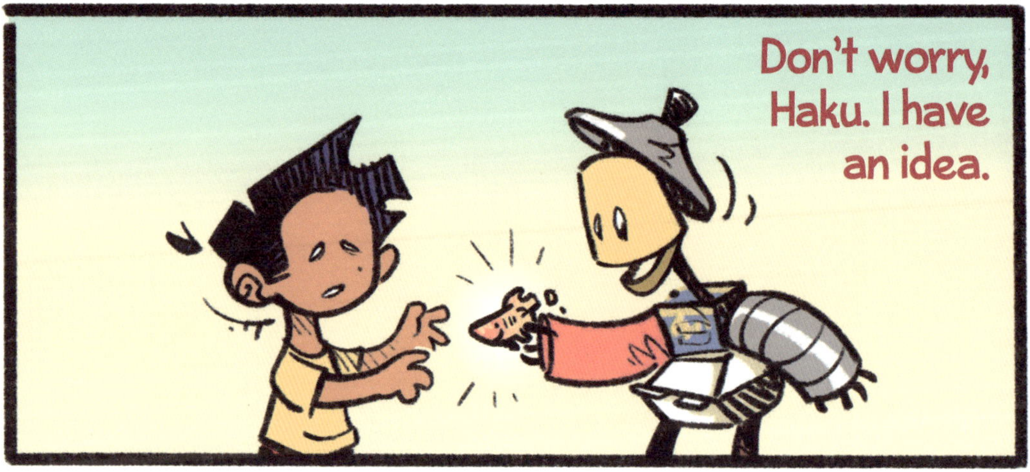
Don't worry, Haku. I have an idea.

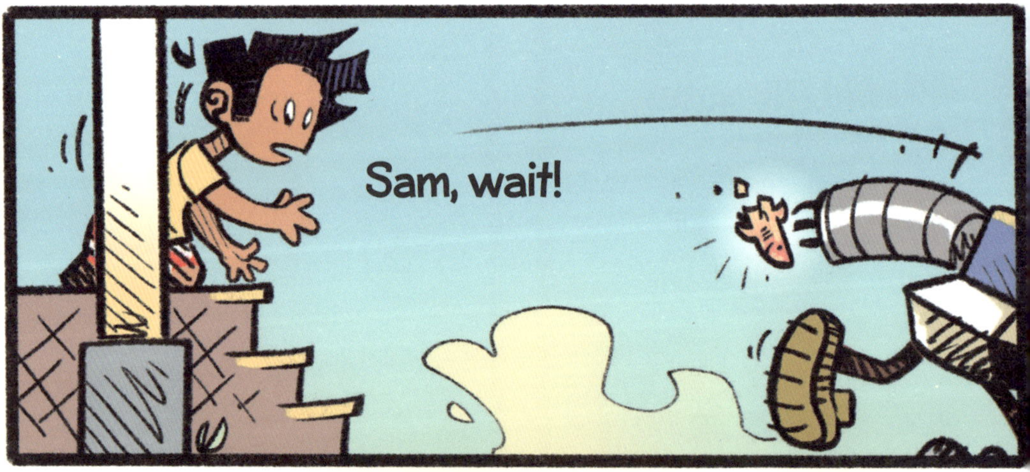
Sam, wait!

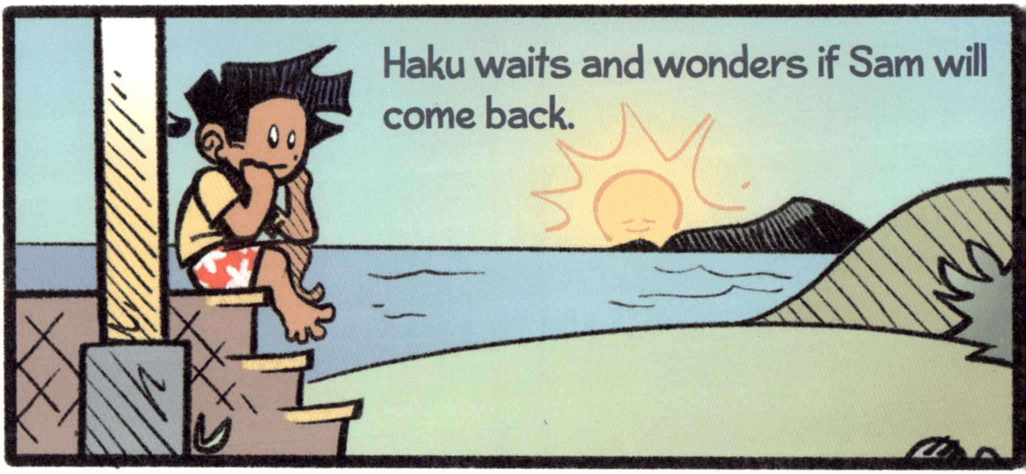
Haku waits and wonders if Sam will come back.

chapter six

BACK HOME

After a while, Sam returns
with a gift for Haku.

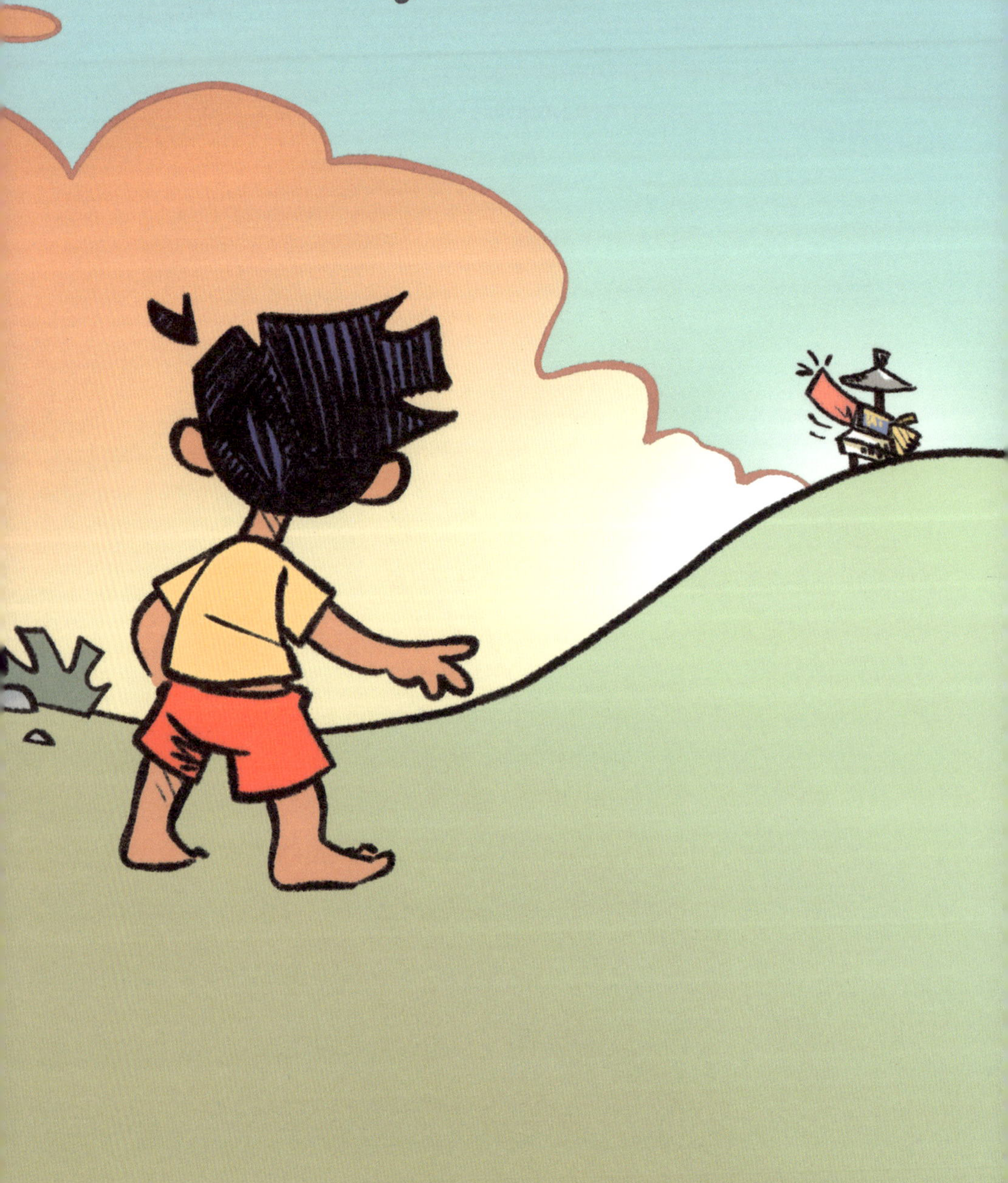

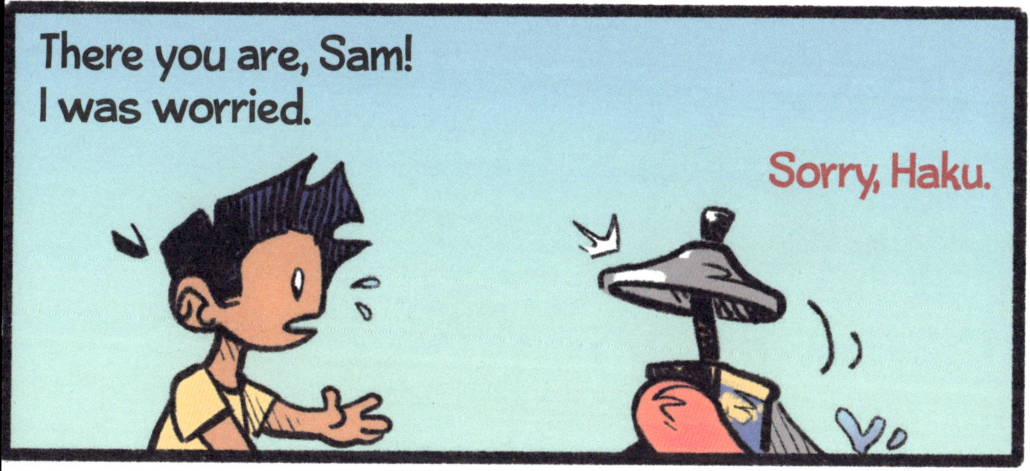
There you are, Sam!
I was worried.
Sorry, Haku.

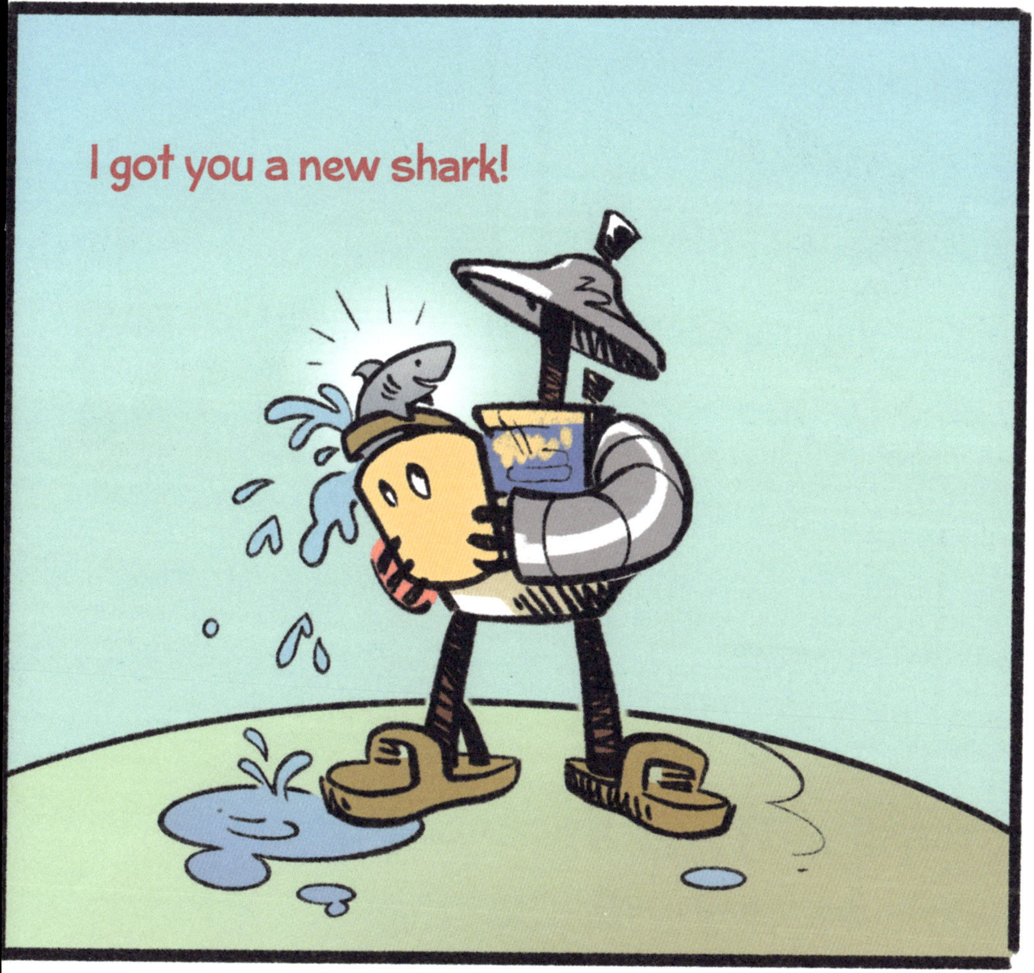
I got you a new shark!

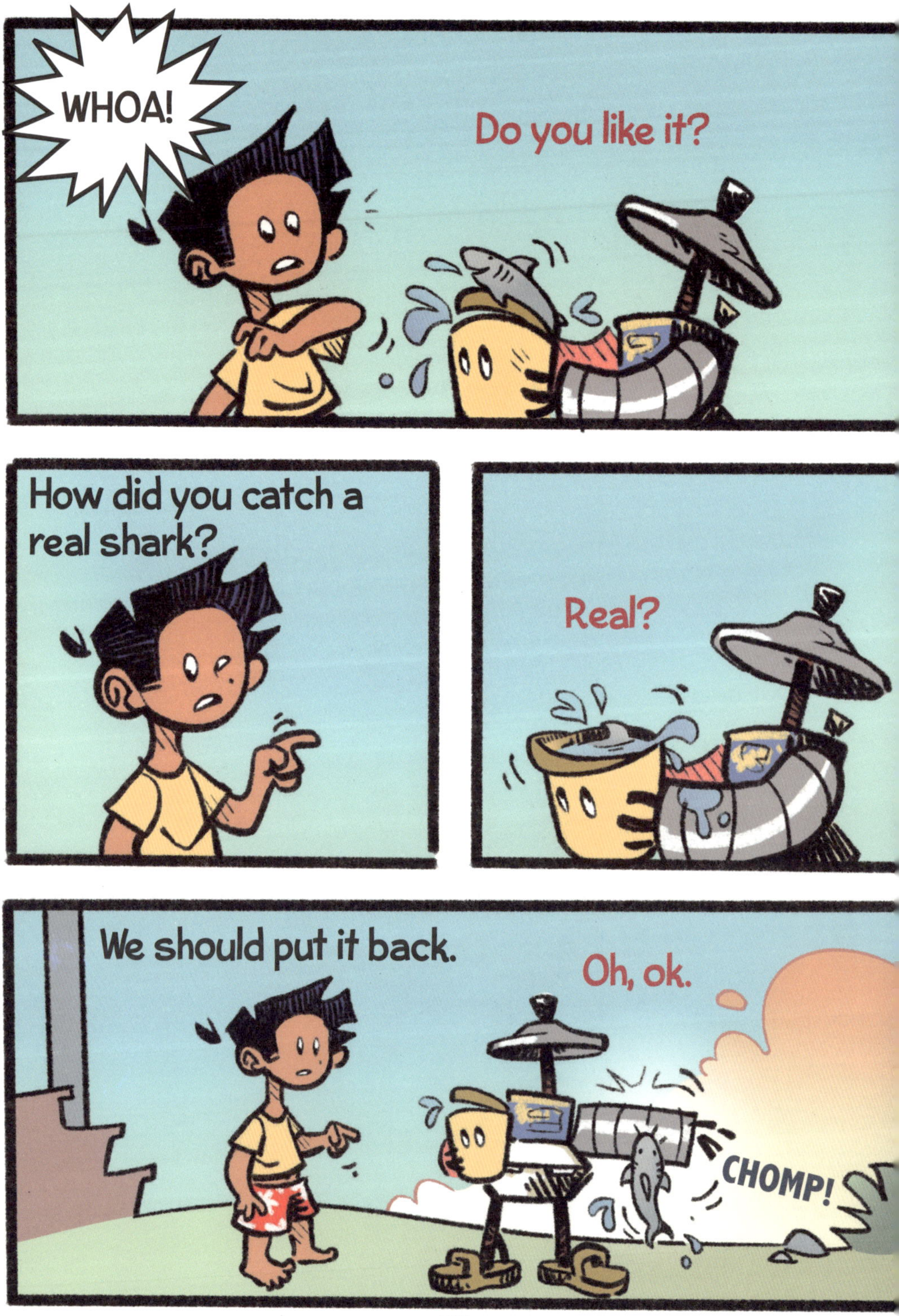

WHOA!
Do you like it?
How did you catch a real shark?
Real?
We should put it back.
Oh, ok.
CHOMP!

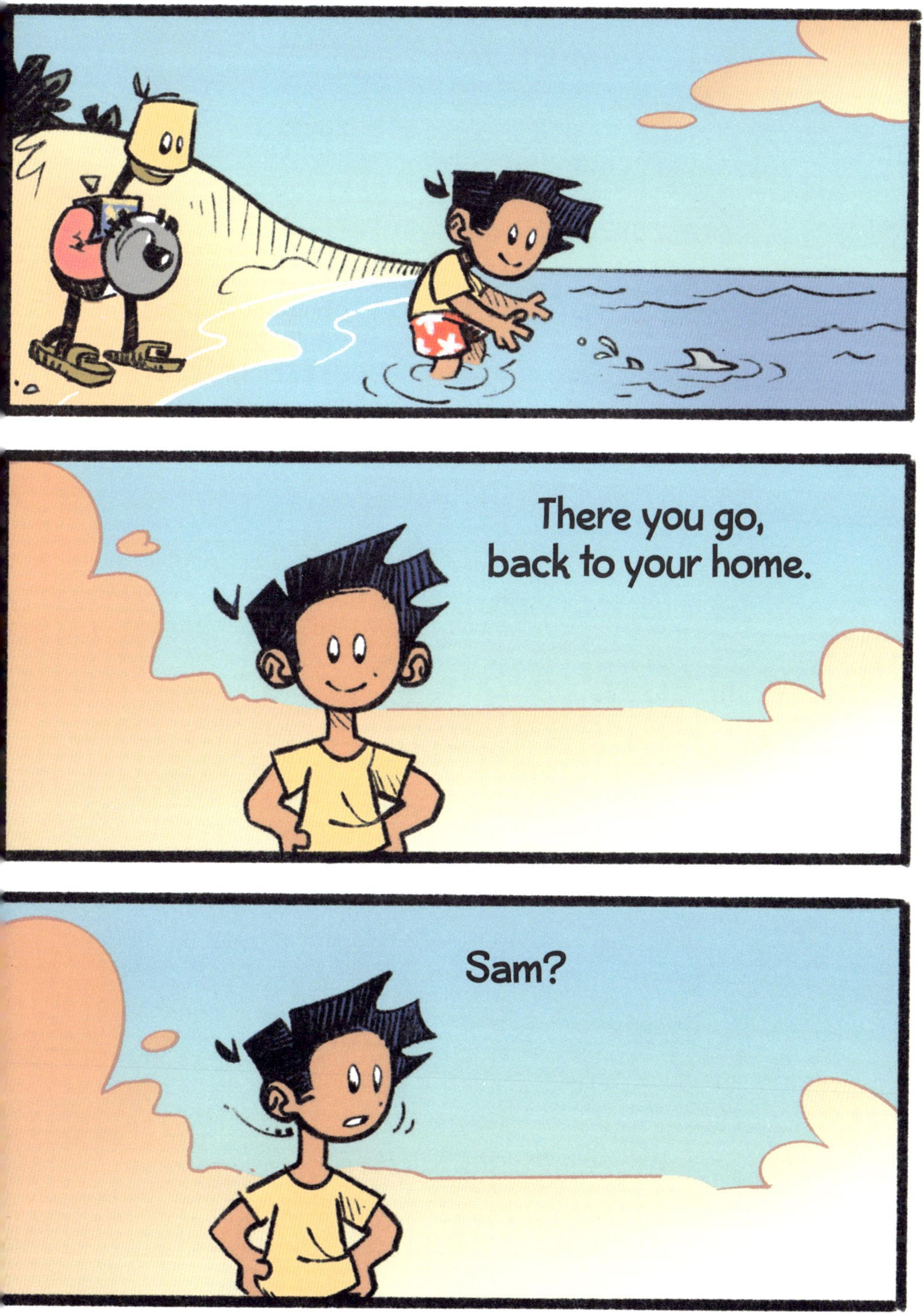
There you go, back to your home.
Sam?

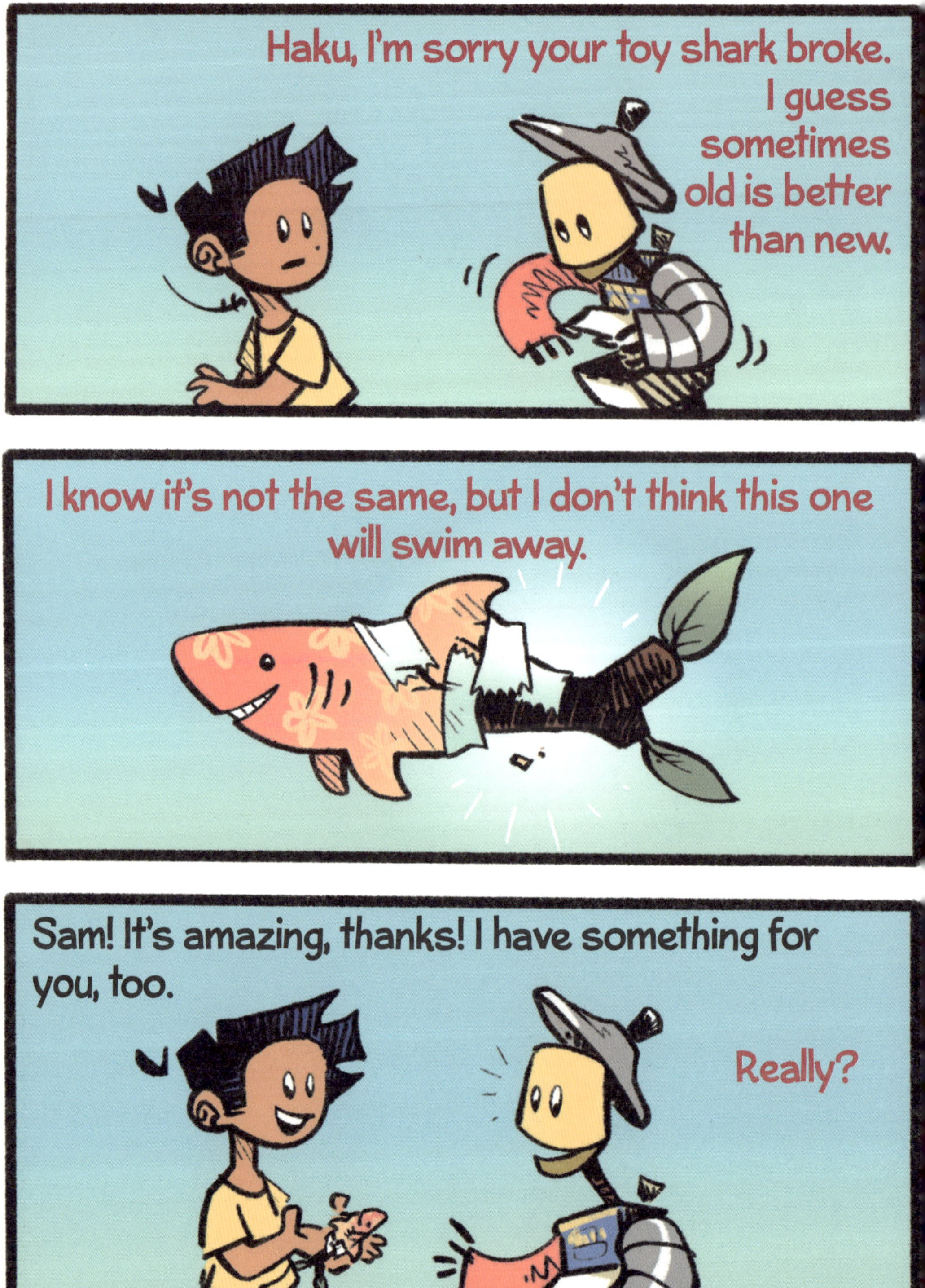
Haku, I'm sorry your toy shark broke. I guess sometimes old is better than new.
I know it's not the same, but I don't think this one will swim away.
Sam! It's amazing, thanks! I have something for you, too.
Really?

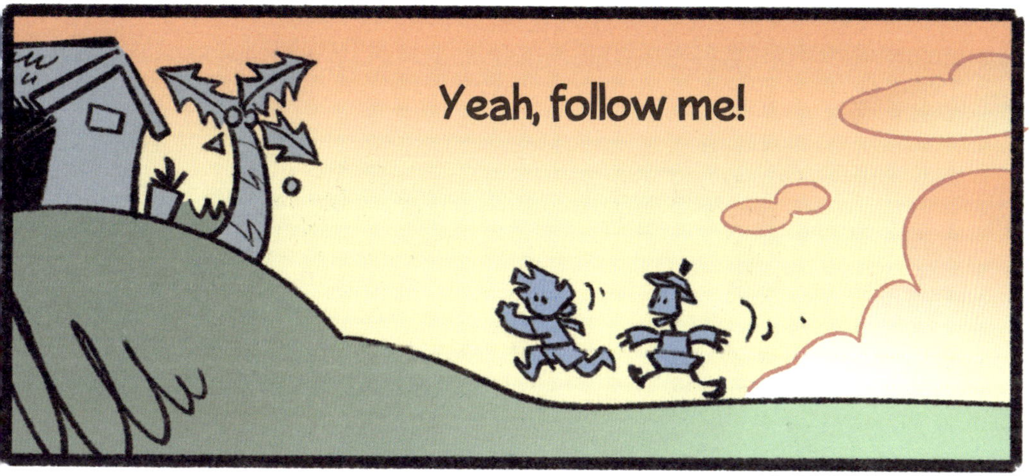
Yeah, follow me!

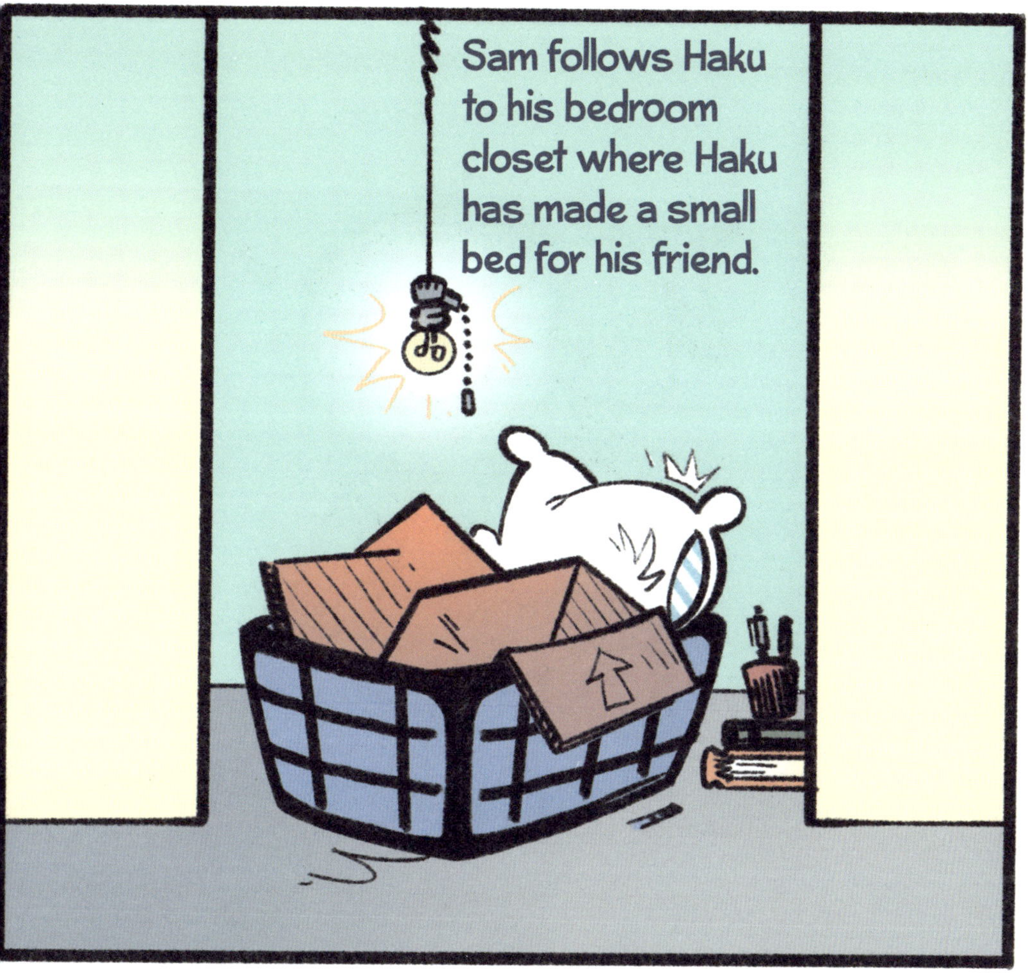
Sam follows Haku to his bedroom closet where Haku has made a small bed for his friend.

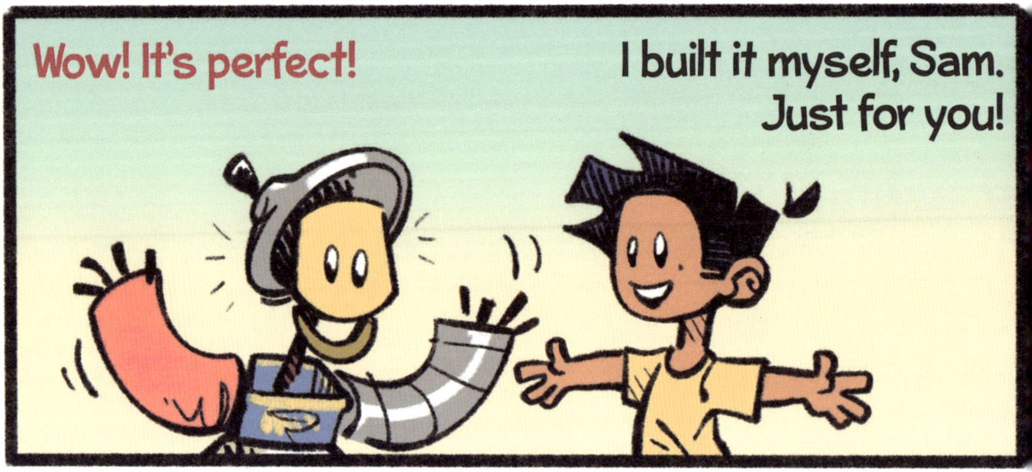
Wow! It's perfect!
I built it myself, Sam. Just for you!

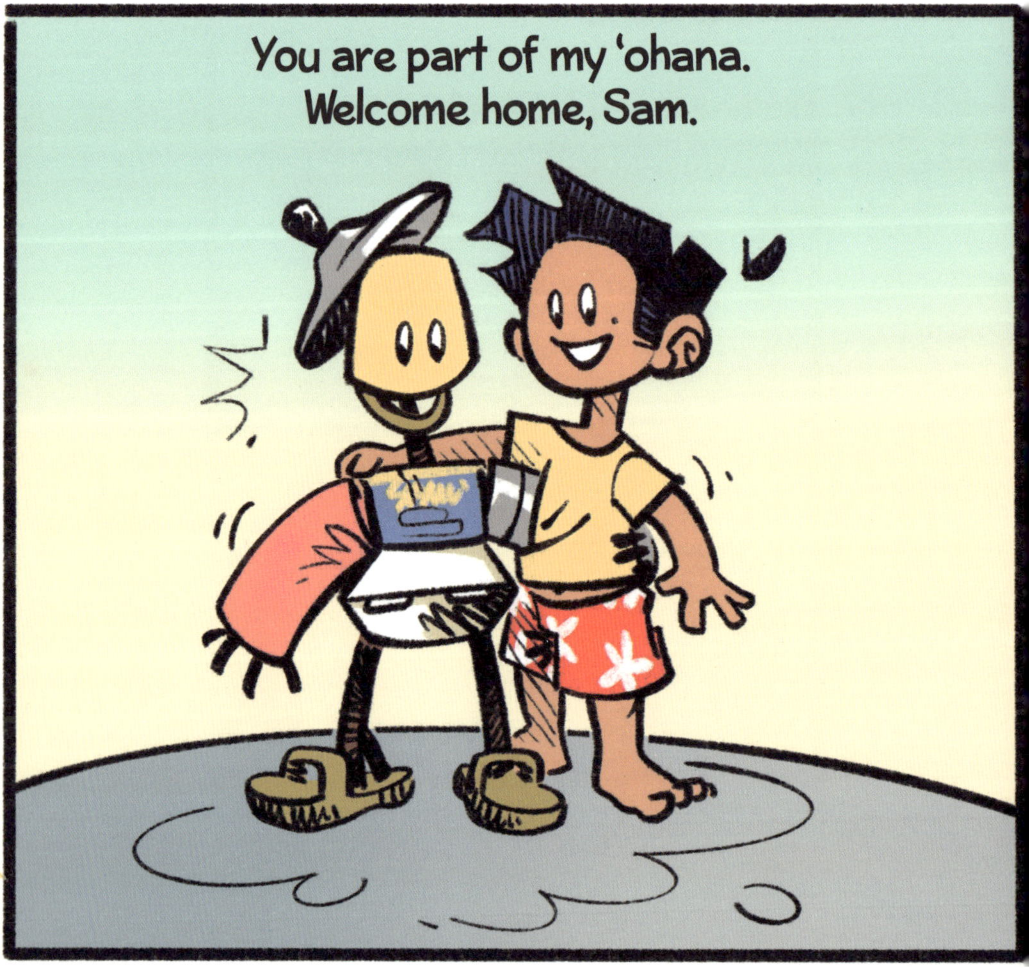
You are part of my 'ohana. Welcome home, Sam.

As night falls and the stars shine above the island, Haku and Sam sleep soundly and dream of tomorrow's adventures.

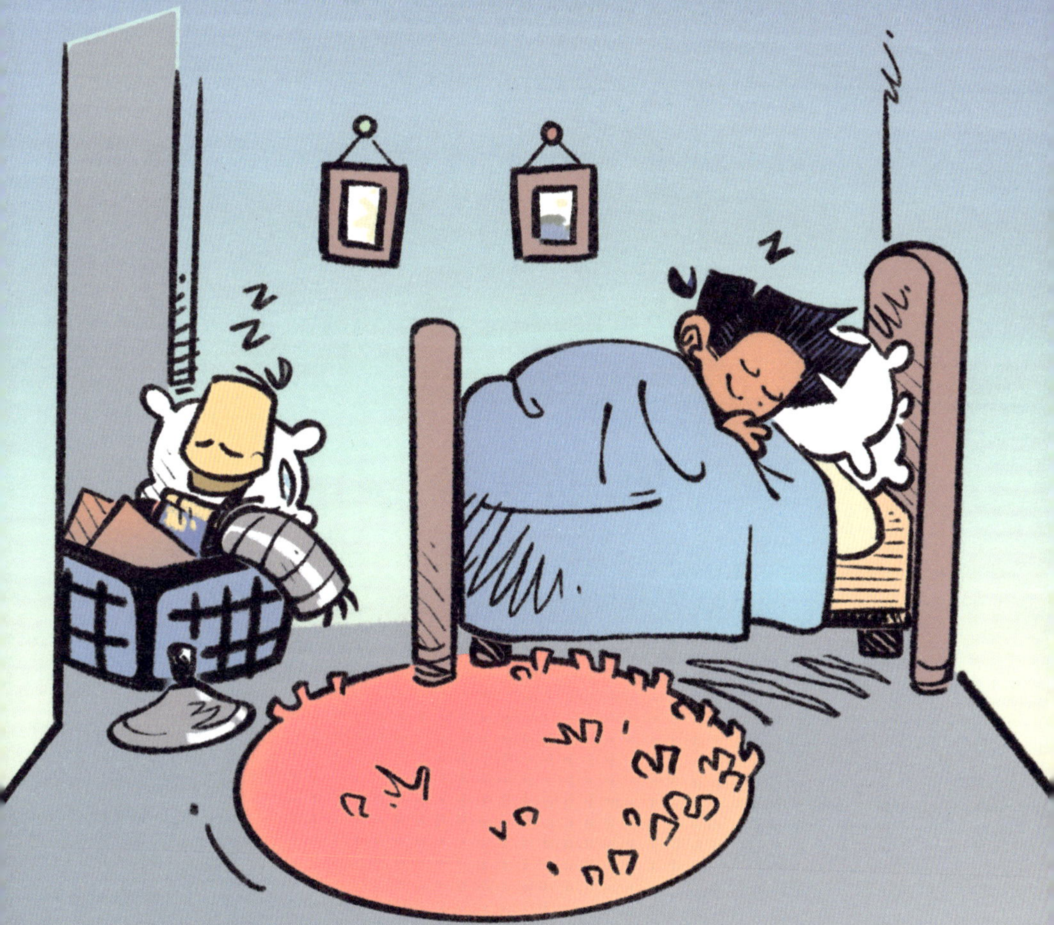
Z
Z
Z
Z

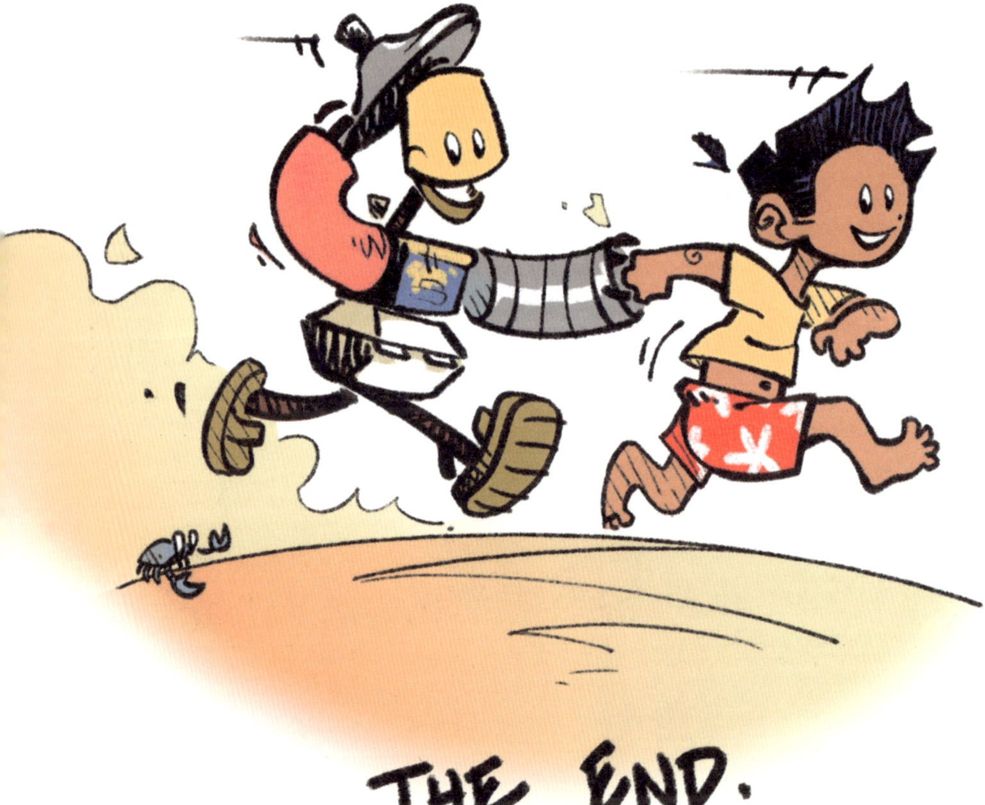

THE END.

About the Author-Illustrator

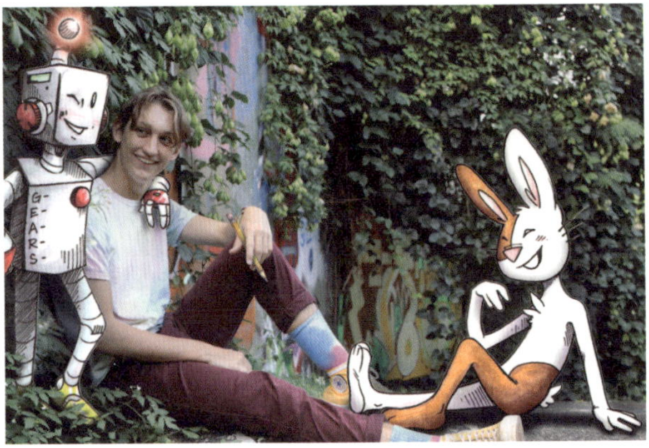
G-
E-
A-
R-
S-

Shane Petosa-Sigel was born in Seattle in 2000 and moved to the island of O'ahu with his family when he was two years old. Not remembering much from the mainland, he has grown up in Kailua his entire life and has comfortably called it home.

Since he was a child, Shane has been drawing comics, writing stories, and creating fictitious worlds to roam. Math homework was often turned in with scribbles and characters living between the margins, notebooks soon became sketchbooks, and the first iterations of many imaginary worlds were realized through countless class notes and scrap papers along the way.

As he has gotten older, he has found that the importance of an active imagination has only intensified and that it is a gift lost by many as they enter adulthood. Shane continues to practice and refine his love for comics and storytelling, and hopes that his stories can foster the imaginations of many young readers and rekindle a lost spark in their parents as well.

In February of 2020, he released the first issue of his own comic book series, "The Shaneivurse," at the Amazing Comic-Con Aloha in Honolulu. Shane has started several other projects as well, including his partnership with Beachhouse Publishing to create his first children's graphic novel, *Haku and Sam.*

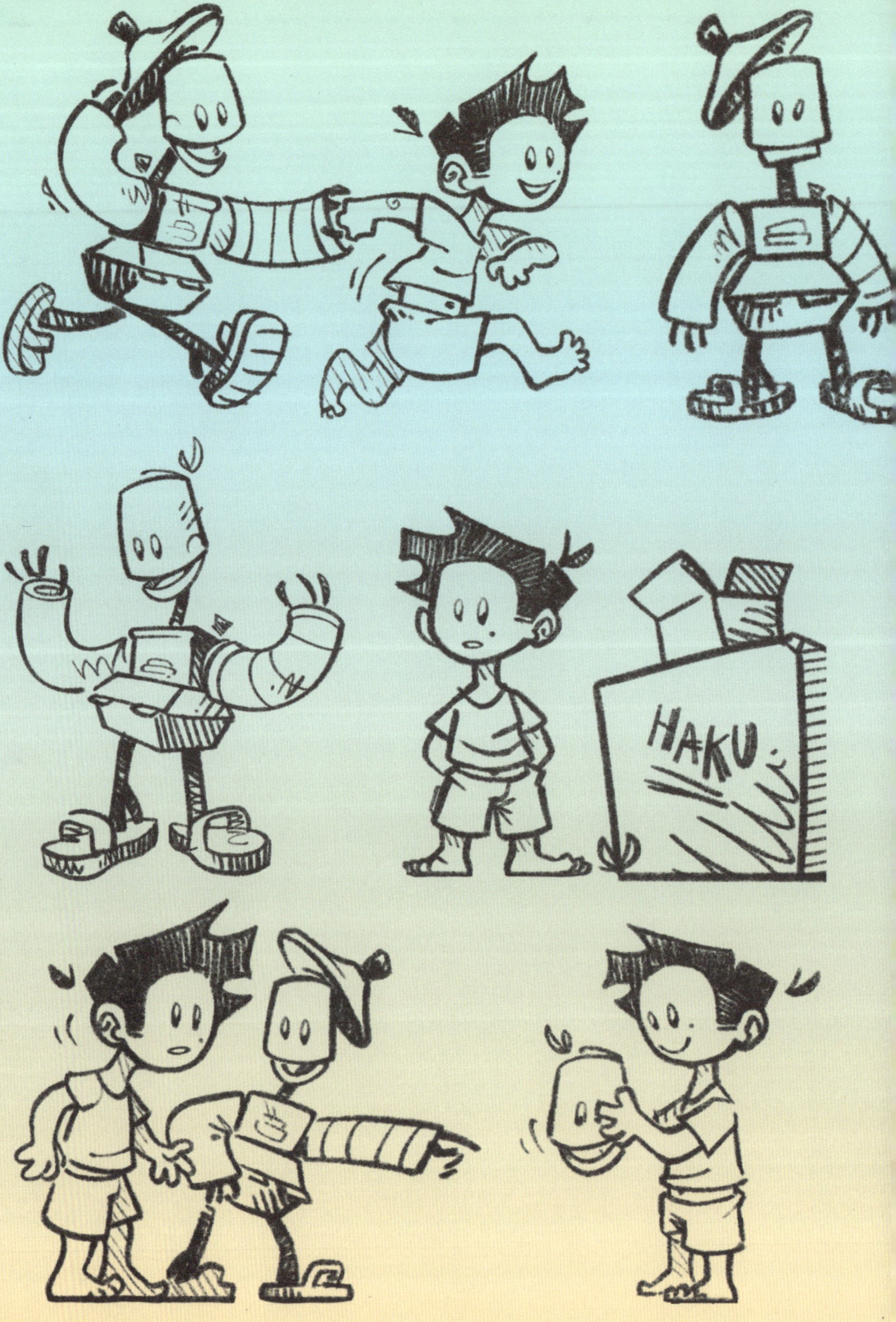
HAKU